"IT'S BEEN A LONG TIME, CIMARRON."

"I was all the way out in No Man's Land, honey. Getting there and getting back here took a whole lot of time, some of which I'd've much rather spent in bed with you."

"I bought a new mattress out of my savings," Marcie confided conspiratorially. "It's stuffed with one hundred percent goosedown. It's so soft, Cimarron, that you think you're floating on a cloud when you sink down on it."

Cimarron stepped closer to Marcie. "When I sink down next to you, honey, I could be in a bed with a mattress on it that's made of bricks but I'd never even notice on account of *you're* so soft. Tell you what. When I come by to see you tonight, let's you and me try . . ." He cupped her ear in both of his hands and whispered into it. . . .

CIMARRON
AND THE VIGILANTES

Ø

SIGNET Westerns You'll Enjoy

CIMARRON

AND THE VIGILANTES

BY

LEO P. KELLEY

A SIGNET BOOK

NEW AMERICAN LIBRARY

PUBLISHER'S NOTE

This novel is a work of fiction. Names, characters, places, and incidents either are the product of the author's imagination or are used fictitiously, and any resemblance to actual persons, living or dead, or events, is entirely coincidental.

NAL BOOKS ARE AVAILABLE AT QUANTITY DISCOUNTS WHEN USED TO PROMOTE PRODUCTS OR SERVICES. FOR INFORMATION PLEASE WRITE TO PREMIUM MARKETING DIVISION, NEW AMERICAN LIBRARY, 1633 BROADWAY, NEW YORK, NEW YORK 10019.

The first chapter of this book appeared in *Cimarron in No Man's Land*, the eighth volume of this series.

SIGNET TRADEMARK REG. U.S. PAT. OFF. AND FOREIGN COUNTRIES
REGISTERED TRADEMARK—MARCA REGISTRADA
HECHO EN CHICAGO, U.S.A.

SIGNET, SIGNET CLASSIC, MENTOR, PLUME, MERIDIAN AND NAL BOOKS are published by New American Library, 1633 Broadway, New York, New York 10019

First Printing, May, 1984

1 2 3 4 5 6 7 8 9

PRINTED IN THE UNITED STATES OF AMERICA

CIMARRON . . .

. . . he was a man with a past he wanted to forget and a future uncertain at best and dangerous at worst. Men feared and secretly admired him. Women desired him. He roamed the Indian Territory with a Winchester '73 in his saddle scabbard, an Army Colt in his hip holster, and a bronc he had broken beneath him. He packed his guns loose, rode his horse hard, and no one dared throw gravel in his boots. Once he had an ordinary name like other men. But a tragic killing forced him to abandon it and he became known only as Cimarron. *Cimarron*, in Spanish, meant wild and unruly. It suited him. *Cimarron*.

1

When the ferry docked on the eastern bank of the Arkansas River, Cimarron led the pack of almost two dozen deputies who dashed ashore.

They went hooting and hollering along the grimy Fort Smith waterfront, heading south past the saloons and whorehouses lining the river's bank.

"We need a name," one of the deputies in the mob called out. "Something slick to make our team official."

"How about the Rounders, Simpson?" one of the deputies proposed to the man who had spoken.

"That's not the name of a team," Simpson protested. "That's the name of the game."

A deputy named Horvath spoke up. "Since Cimarron's our team captain and presumably sets an example for all of us, and in consideration of the way he tomcats his way through life, perhaps we ought to call ourselves the Fort Smith Studs."

The deputies responded to Horvath's suggestion with bursts of laughter and lewd remarks directed at the grinning Cimarron.

"How about the Fort Smith Lawmen?" suggested Deputy Deeter.

"What do we need a name for?" Cimarron asked Deeter as he nodded a greeting to the owner of a saloon who stood in the doorway of his establishment, his arms folded and an uneasy expression on his fat face. "Names don't matter all that much. What matters is how well we play."

"Let's have a drink, boys," Simpson suggested. He swerved toward the batwings of the saloon. "We've got some time before the game starts."

"Wait a minute!" cried the owner of the saloon, unfolding his arms and nervously thrusting out both of his hands to block Simpson's approach. "I don't want any trouble. The last time you deputies were in my place it cost me nearly a hundred dollars to repair the damage you caused. Pick someplace else. Please!"

Cimarron went up to the man. "Al, you've got my word. There'll be no fighting this time. We'll behave ourselves. Won't we, boys?"

A chorus of "Sure!" and "You bet!" and "Word of honor, Al!" resounded.

"You could go to Lizzie's place," Al proposed. "It's right down the block there, boys."

But Cimarron and the other deputies ignored the saloon's anxious owner and shouldered their way through the batwings like a herd of bulls smelling water after a month-long drought.

At the bar, Cimarron ordered beer, and when he and the other deputies had all been served, he raised his glass and said, "To victory!"

"To victory!" chorused the deputies.

They drank. So did Cimarron.

"You're being a bit premature, gentlemen," remarked a man with a sallow complexion who was standing at the far end of the bar. "We—the Fort Smith Soldiers—will win the game this afternoon."

"You're sure about that, are you, Bryce?" Cimarron shot back. He drank again, finding the cold beer a welcome relief after the unusual heat of the mid-April day. He studied the man who lived in Fort Smith and who was one of the players on the opposing team.

"Cimarron, you lost the last two games to us," Bryce pointed out matter-of-factly.

"That's true enough, Bryce," Horvath agreed. "But you're forgetting something."

"Forgetting something?" Bryce raised a bushy eyebrow.

"Cimarron wasn't in town when we played you townies the last two times," Horvath stated. "But he's here now and he'll be pitching this afternoon."

"So you'd best throw in the towel right now, Bryce," Simpson declared. "Cimarron will likely bust your boys' bats, the rough way he pitches."

"Simpson," Bryce said, "you're skillful at using that bat you've got swinging between your legs when you're with women, I'm told, but you're not worth a damn on a rounders' diamond."

"Why, you sarcastic sonofabitch!" Simpson roared, and lunged past Cimarron, heading for Bryce.

"Oh, no!" moaned Al, twisting his hands helplessly together. "Oh, sweet Jesus, no!"

Simpson seized Bryce by the throat with both of his huge hands and began to throttle the man. Bryce swiftly brought up one knee and slammed it into Simpson's groin, breaking the deputy's hold and causing him to bend over and groan as he clutched his genitals. But while still bent over a moment later, Simpson sprang forward and butted Bryce with his head.

"Police!" Al yelled, holding open the batwings. "Po-*lice*!"

Cimarron ran down the length of the bar as Bryce, his fists together and raised above his head, was about to bring them down against the back of the still-doubled-over Simpson's skull. He shoved Simpson to one side and threw a right cross that slammed Bryce back against the wall, knocking the wind from his lungs.

"That's enough!" he told Simpson, who had straightened up and was glaring at Bryce. "Bryce, you don't want any more trouble from this hotheaded deputy friend of mine, now do you?" He turned to Simpson. "Simpson, why is it you fly off the handle whenever you think somebody's insulting you? Bryce wasn't insulting you. He was paying you a compliment.

He said he'd heard of your nearly worldwide reputation as a ladies' man.''

Bryce's fist flew but Cimarron had seen it coming out of the corner of his eye. He threw up his left arm and deflected the blow. Then he threw a right uppercut that split Bryce's lower lip.

"You want to knuckle and skull it, Bryce," he said, "I'm game." He stood, his hands fisted in front of him, his green eyes boring into Bryce's.

Bryce raised a hand to his bleeding lip, withdrew it, looked at the blood on his fingers and then at Cimarron before striding swiftly from the saloon.

"What's the trouble?" asked one of the officers of Fort Smith's police force as he entered the saloon and suspiciously surveyed the men in it.

"No trouble, officer," Cimarron said mildly. "Just some high spirits on the part of these deputies here."

"Al's a nervous man," Horvath commented. "He thought we were fixing to have ourselves a fight."

"But we fight crime," the deputy named Deeter said innocently, "not each other."

The policeman gave Al a questioning glance.

Al looked over at Cimarron and then back at the policeman. "I guess I was a mite apprehensive, officer. I guess I shouldn't have called for the police."

The policeman gave the deputies gathered at the bar a cynically appraising glance and then left the saloon.

"Have another beer, Cimarron," Deeter said. "I'll buy."

"If you're buying, then I'm not refusing." Cimarron returned to his former place at the bar.

"Let's take a vote," one of the deputies proposed.

"On what?" Cimarron inquired as he drank some of his second beer.

"Our name. Deeter suggested the Fort Smith Lawmen. Somebody else suggested the Fort Smith Studs and—''

Cimarron's arm shot out. He seized the hat of the deputy who had been speaking and pulled it down over the man's eyes.

The deputy calmly pushed it back up again. "Anybody else got any more suggestions?"

"We have to be fast on our feet in this job," Deeter mused, "and even faster on the draw sometimes. How about the Gunslingers?"

The suggestion was greeted with cheers. A vote on the proposed names for the team was quickly taken and the deputies chose to dub themselves the Gunslingers by a margin of seventeen to four.

Then, at a silent signal from Cimarron, the Gunslingers left the saloon—to Al's immense and visible relief—on their way to play a game of rounders against the townies' team, the Fort Smith Soldiers.

Pummeling each other playfully and good-naturedly joking at each other's expense, they made their rambunctious way south through the town until they reached the flat bluff overlooking the Poteau River at the point where it joined the Arkansas River.

Cimarron whistled through his teeth and shook his head in mock dismay.

"What's the matter?" Deeter asked him.

Cimarron pointed at the men of the townies' team, who stood swinging bats and tossing balls back and forth between them. "I declare," he said, "it's a sight to scar a man's eyes and leave him about blinded the way those dandies do strut about in those costumes of theirs. Compared to them, we look like something the cat dragged in."

He surveyed the uniforms of the Fort Smith Soldiers' team: bib shirts made of red silk, black-belted white flannel knickerbockers, knee-high black socks, low-cut shoes and round visored caps with two broad red stripes circling them.

"Let's go over and have a friendly word with our competition," Simpson suggested, beginning to cross the diamond to where the Soldiers were gathered.

"That's fraternizing with the enemy!" cried Horvath, assuming a shocked expression before smiling and following Simpson and the others. "Come on, Cimarron!" he yelled, looking back over his shoulder.

"Be with you in a minute," Cimarron called back, his eyes on a woman standing in the front of the crowd that had gathered to watch the game, a frilly pink parasol raised above her head to shield her from the rays of the hot afternoon sun.

He walked across the field past third base and, when he reached the woman who was watching him approach, tilted his hat back on his head, thrust his thumbs into his belt and said, "Marcie, it's good to see you again."

"I heard you were back in town," Marcie said in a sweet but slightly husky voice. "I'd hoped you'd come to visit me. But since you didn't, I decided to come out here to see you."

"You're looking as fine and fashionable as ever, Marcie."

"Why didn't you come to see me, Cimarron?"

"Just got back day before yesterday and, truth to tell, I was bushed. After I turned my prisoners over to Charley Burns and filled out all the papers he handed me, I took the ferry back across the Arkansas and practically fell asleep on my feet before I even got to my tepee on the deputies' campground over there. And there I've been, asleep most of the time, since.

"But I don't expect to be bushed tonight. I'll come by Mrs. Windham's parlor house and see if you're free. You are working tonight?"

"I am and I'll be free. Even if Mrs. Windham has men standing in line to—uh, be with me, I'll be sure to be free when you arrive. It's been a long time, Cimarron."

"I was all the way out in No Man's Land, honey. Getting there and then getting back here took a whole lot of time, some of which I'd've much rather spent in bed with you."

"I bought a new mattress out of my savings," Marcie confided conspiratorially. "It's stuffed with one hundred percent goose down. It's so soft, Cimarron, that you think you're floating on a cloud when you sink down on it."

Cimarron stepped closer to Marcie. "When I sink down on you, honey, I could be on a mattress that's made of bricks but I'd never even notice on account of *you're* so soft. Tell you what. When I come by to see you tonight, let's you and me try doing it—'' He cupped her ear in both of his hands and whispered into it.

"That's impossible! Nobody could do it that way!"

"Want to bet?"

"You have?"

He nodded. Grinned.

"Oh, my goodness!" Marcie exclaimed, and her parasol began to flutter. "But I'm the one who should be teaching you tricks like that. I am, after all, a working woman. A professional woman."

"When you try what we're going to do together tonight on some of your other customers, they'll think that both Sodom and Gomorrah have gone and engulfed Fort Smith."

"Cimarron, that's the *truth!*"

"Cimarron!" Deeter yelled from across the field. "Let's go, man!"

"Be seeing you," Cimarron told Marcie.

"Tonight," she breathed before he left her and hurried across the field to where his teammates were waiting for him.

A shrill whistle sounded as he joined the other Gunslingers and they, like the spectators and the members of the Soldiers' team, turned their attention to the frock-coated man who had just blown the whistle.

He took it from his mouth as silence descended on the crowd, cleared his throat and announced, "Ladies and gentlemen, I am pleased to inform you that the merchants of Fort Smith have, each and every one of them, contributed to a fund which has been used to purchase two kegs of beer which will both be awarded to the winners of today's game of rounders!"

"Mighty generous," Cimarron murmured. "Though I reckon I could polish off one of those kegs all by myself."

"The prize for the winners," continued the whistle blower, "is given in appreciation of the friendly contest and competitive spirit of the two teams who meet here today to provide us all with some wholesome entertainment." The official representative of the town's merchants ha-haed and then he harumphed. "That is all I have to say, ladies and gentlemen. Let the game begin!"

"The Fort Smith Soldiers," shouted a rotund little man who had been designated the game's umpire, "will bat first! Deputies, take the field!"

"Gunslingers!" Horvath yelled.

"Beg pardon?" The fat little umpire peered at Horvath, one hand above his eyes to shield them from the glare of the sun.

"As of today, we're the Gunslingers," Horvath explained before running with Cimarron and his other teammates to take up their positions on the diamond.

The Soldiers stationed themselves behind home plate.

The umpire shouted, "Play ball!"

Cimarron, on the pitching mound, watched the first batter take several practice swings with his bat. When the man, knees bent and bat over his right shoulder was ready, Cimarron threw the game's first ball.

"Strike!" the umpire declared as the ball went in under the Soldier's bat. Deeter caught it and threw it back to Cimarron.

The Soldier connected with Cimarron's next pitch, which was high and outside. He dropped his bat and ran but was not even halfway to first base when the umpire called a foul. Minutes later, he had struck out.

The next batter connected on Cimarron's first pitch and made it to second base before the Gunslinger playing left field got the ball to the second baseman.

Cimarron, as Bryce stepped up to home plate, turned away from the man and surreptitiously spit on the ball. Turning back, he drew back his right arm, his left leg rising from the ground as he did so, and then sent his spitball barreling toward Bryce, who, he had noticed, looked none the worse for the fracas in the saloon.

"Strike!" the umpire declared.

Cimarron threw again.

Bryce bunted.

Cimarron sprang forward, scooped up the ball and threw to third base.

14

"Out!" the umpire announced as the third baseman threw to first. "Out!" he announced again.

"Double play!" a man in the crowd yelled happily, and others cheered as an obviously disconsolate Bryce and the Soldier who had tried to make it from second to third walked back behind home plate.

As the game continued the Soldiers put a man on third and one on second.

Cimarron hefted the ball in his hand, pulled his hat down low on his forehead and went for a strike against the batter facing him. But the man's bat slammed against the ball and the high fly went soaring through the air. Simpson, in right field, raced after and under it, his eager hands reaching up. But he stumbled. The ball eluded his grasp and fell to the ground. He bent down, grabbed it and threw it to the third baseman.

But the Soldiers on second and third made it home to the delighted shouts of the spectators, and when the inning ended some time later, the Soldiers were leading by a score of two to zero.

Cimarron, standing behind the Soldier who was catching, cheered with his teammates as Horvath, the first man up for the Gunslingers, hit a home run on Bryce's first low and inside pitch.

Simpson, up next, struck out. Swearing, he stepped aside and handed his bat to Deeter, who racked up four balls and walked.

When it was Cimarron's turn to bat, Deeter had stolen second base and was trying to steal third but Bryce, before pitching to Cimarron, halted Deeter by throwing to third base. The third baseman threw to second and Deeter was barely safe as a result of a long dusty slide.

Bryce turned his attention to Cimarron. He wound up and pitched a curve ball.

Cimarron swung and the umpire yelled, "Strike!"

"Ball!" the umpire yelled on Bryce's next pitch.

There was the ghost of a grin on Bryce's face as he prepared to pitch to Cimarron a third time.

Moments later, as the ball came flying toward him Cimarron dropped his bat and tried to step back out of the ball's path, but he failed to move fast enough and the ball struck him in the ribs on the left side. It sent pain shooting up his spine and forced a curse from between his lips.

"You all right?" asked a deputy who was standing behind him.

"You did that deliberate, Bryce!" Cimarron yelled, one hand clutching his burning ribs. "In my book, Bryce, you are one bona-fide bastard!"

"*Play Ball!*" the umpire called out in an uncertain voice, his uneasy eyes darting back and forth between Cimarron and Bryce.

Cimarron strode toward the pitching mound, and as he did so Bryce began to shake his head and back away from him. Cimarron quickened his pace, and as Bryce continued to back even more swiftly away from him he broke into a sprint. A moment later, he had his hands on Bryce and was muttering, "You do that again, Bryce, and I'll stuff a bat so far down your throat it'll come out your ass!"

Bryce kicked Cimarron in the shin and tried to break away from him.

"Did you see that?" an enraged Simpson yelled from beside home plate. He went running out onto the field, his teammates racing right behind him.

As an equally enraged Cimarron gave Bryce a left jab and then a hard right uppercut and Bryce delivered a badly aimed blow that bounced off Cimarron's shoulder, the Soldiers left the field and the bases and came running toward Cimarron and Bryce, who had fallen to the ground and were now rolling over and over in a cloud of dust.

The Soldiers and Gunslingers reached the combatants at the same time as the crowd watched in silence. Horvath reached down to pull Bryce away from Cimarron, but as he did so one of the Soldiers threw a left that knocked him to the ground. Simpson downed the man who had downed Horvath and was given a crushing blow in the gut by the Soldiers' first baseman.

The melee quickly grew into a free-for-all and the crowd,

16

now cheering lustily, surged forward to form a wide circle around the battling men.

Bryce, beneath Cimarron, reached up, got the palm of one hand under his opponent's chin and began to push Cimarron's head back. At the same time, he tried with his free hand to claw at Cimarron's eyes but Cimarron swatted the man's hand away and then sprang to his feet. He was about to reach down for Bryce when a Soldier landed on his back. He bent down and threw the man over his head.

When the Soldier landed on top of Bryce, a hand grabbed Cimarron's shoulder from behind and spun him around. Cimarron blocked the blow and delivered a series of punishing body blows that effectively neutralized his attacker.

Then, as battling bodies swirled around him, he found himself down on the ground again, struck by a man he didn't see who had slammed into him after being punched by Deeter.

A whistle began to blow, and as he got to his feet again and shoved a Soldier out of his way Cimarron realized that it was the town official, the representative of the merchants who had donated the two kegs of beer, who was frantically whistling as if the sound he was making would in some mysterious and perhaps magical way halt the violent battle that was being waged on the diamond.

A Soldier hurtled past Cimarron, spinning, a silk-shirted red blur.

Dust eddied up from the ground and Cimarron, choking on it, his eyes smarting, blinked. A soldier's hard fist smashed into the side of his head and he staggered forward to collide with Simpson, who yelled, "This beats playing rounders, don't it, Cimarron?"

Before Cimarron could answer, a Soldier lunged at him, the man's arms reaching for him, his face twisted into a hard mask of unrestrained anger. Cimarron ducked and went in under the man's reaching arms. He picked the man up and hurled him, howling, into one of his teammates who was about to club Horvath with a bat. The Soldier went down, taking his teammate with him. Cimarron ran up to both men, grabbed their silk shirts, hauled them to their feet and resoundingly cracked their skulls together. Both men gave sibilant sighs and, when Cimarron released them, crumpled unconscious to the ground.

Cimarron, breathing fast, looked around and realized that some of the townies had joined the fight. When one of them bent down and picked up the bat that Horvath's attacker had dropped and raised it high above a groggy Deeter's head, Cimarron moved in on the man, tore the bat from his hands and threw it away. He buried his right fist in the man's flabby gut, dropping the would-be attacker. Then he raised his right leg and sent it shooting out at a right angle to his body. His boot hit an oncoming Soldier's hip. The man dropped the keg of beer he had been holding over his head as a potentially lethal weapon and he and it hit the ground hard, the keg splintering upon impact to send its sudsy contents spraying on the fighting men nearby and on the Soldier bellowing in pain.

Cimarron flexed his aching fingers. He stood panting in the dust through which men were moving like agitated apparitions. He put up one hand and gingerly touched his temple where the Soldier's fist had landed, and felt the warm sticky blood covering the spot.

"Look out, Cimarron!" Simpson yelled from somewhere in the distance.

He turned quickly to find a Soldier racing toward him with a flat stone that had been one of the bases in his hands. He swiftly sidestepped, put out one booted foot and tripped the man, who, as he pitched forward on his face, Cimarron recognized as the husband of a woman in Fort Smith with whom he had once been friendly. Too friendly, he recalled, as the woman's husband, who now lay dazed at his feet, had once loudly informed him.

He was grinning when the shot sounded. He squinted into the dust, searching for the man who had fired the shot.

Then another shot sounded.

The official's whistle shrieked. The umpire scurried through the dust shouting, "Order, gentlemen, *please*!"

The Soldiers, Gunslingers and the townies were suddenly

frozen in crouching positions or with their fists drawn back, their faces contorted with rage.

"That's just about enough of this foolishness, dammit!" a male voice thundered, and then its owner emerged from the dust and Cimarron recognized Ralph Fanton, one of Charley Burns's assistant jailers.

As a Gunslinger suddenly lunged at a Soldier, Fanton fired over the deputy's head and the Gunslinger halted in midstride, his fists dropping to his sides as he stared apprehensively at Fanton.

"Cimarron," Fanton said in a disgusted tone, "don't you have anything better to do than this?"

"Not at the moment, Ralph."

"You're wrong," Fanton snapped. "You do have something better to do."

"I do?"

"Damn right you do. Marshal Upham sent me out here to get you and bring you back to his office. He wants to have a talk with you."

"What about?"

"How the hell should I know what about?"

Marcie came running out of the crowd and up to Cimarron. She threw her arms around his neck. "Are you hurt? Oh, Cimarron, you *are* hurt!" she wailed when she saw his injured temple.

"I'll be all right, honey," he assured her.

She released him and then took his hand. "You're coming back to Mrs. Windham's with me right this minute. I'll clean your wound and bandage it for you. Are you sure your skull's not fractured?"

"It's far too thick to fracture," Fanton muttered.

"Let's go, Cimarron," Marcie said as she tried to lead him off the field that was being deserted by the players and spectators.

"Begging your pardon, Miss Marcie," Fanton said firmly. "Cimarron's coming with me. Business before pleasure."

Marcie glanced at Cimarron who shrugged.

Then, as he followed Fanton off the field, he looked longingly back over his shoulder at Marcie.

"I guess I got to thank you, Marshal," Cimarron said as he walked through the open door into Marshal D. P. Upham's office in the Fort Smith courthouse.

Upham made no response to the remark and Cimarron halted in the middle of the room and stood staring at the marshal's back.

Upham was standing at the window, his hands clasped behind him, his head bowed.

"If you hadn't've sent for me, Marshal," Cimarron said, deciding to try again for a response, "I might well be dead by now. That game of rounders we were playing this afternoon got a bit out of hand, you might say."

Did Upham sigh? Cimarron wasn't sure.

The marshal turned away from the window and, without looking in Cimarron's direction, walked over to his desk and sat down behind it. He gestured peremptorily, still without looking at Cimarron, and Cimarron sat down in a chair facing the desk.

"You got a case for me, have you, Marshal?"

This time Cimarron was sure. Marshal Upham had definitely sighed.

The lawman's hands lay flat upon an envelope, which was the only item visible on the top of his usually hopelessly cluttered desk. Without looking up at Cimarron, he said, "You and Deputy Sean Cassidy were friends."

Cimarron's eyes narrowed. He wondered if he had been asked a question or if Upham had merely made a statement of fact. "We were."

"You two worked on the Matlock case together, as I recall, among others."

"We did. We watched Matlock hang for butchering his baby boy."

"Cassidy was a good man."

Was?

"What's eating at you, Marshal?"

20

Upham raised a hand and ran his fingers through his thinning hair.

"Something sure is, Marshal. You want to let me in on it?"

Upham looked up at Cimarron, who noticed the mixture of weariness and sadness in the man's eyes. "I have an assignment for you."

"It's got something to do with Cassidy?"

Upham nodded. He looked down at the already opened envelope lying on his desk and then he gingerly picked it up as if he were afraid it might contaminate him. "Cassidy's dead."

Cimarron's body stiffened. His hands tightly gripped his chair's armrests. "Dead?"

Upham leaned over the desk and held the envelope out to Cimarron.

"What's this?" Cimarron asked as he took it. "What happened to Cassidy? How'd he die?"

"He was murdered."

"Who murdered him?"

"He was a damn good deputy," Upham said softly, as if he hadn't heard Cimarron's question.

Cimarron repeated it.

Upham slammed a fist down on his desk and swore. "I don't know who murdered him. But I do know that whoever did it—I want whoever did it, Cimarron, and I want him—or them, as the case may be—badly."

"Somebody shot him?"

Upham shook his head. "That envelope. Open it."

Cimarron did as he was told and removed the only thing the envelope contained—a single photograph. His teeth ground together as he looked down at it. A muscle in his jaw jumped.

He thought of the trails he had traveled with Sean Cassidy. Of the nights around campfires they had shared, the dangers they had faced together and the triumphs they had enjoyed. Cassidy, in Cimarron's mind, smiled his sly Irish smile, slapped him on the back, his bright blue eyes twinkling, the dimples in his ruddy cheeks deepening.

Cimarron's pleasant memories of the times he had shared with Cassidy somersaulted through his mind. A cold fury rose within him as he continued to stare down at the photograph he was holding. A colder hatred flooded him as he thought about the man or men who could have done so savage a thing to his friend. He looked up at Upham, who nodded curtly, wordlessly.

"You'll get whoever did that to Sean," Upham said quietly, and Cimarron had no doubt that the marshal had made a statement of fact this time, had not asked a question.

"I will." Cimarron hesitated, his eyes drawn down again in reluctant fascination to the ugly photograph of Cassidy. He stared at Cassidy's naked and crucified corpse, its bloody hands and feet nailed to two planks that had been crisscrossed and nailed together in the form of an X and then set upright in the ground.

What ground? Where?

"Who sent this to you, Marshal?"

"There was no letter with it. No name on the envelope."

Cimarron picked up the envelope and looked at it. "It's postmarked from Wewoka in Seminole Nation. It's dated April sixteenth—three days ago. Was Cassidy working on a case in Wewoka?"

"No, not as far as I know. He'd gone out after a gang of horse thieves who were reportedly operating near Walnut Creek in Chickasaw Nation. I don't know what he was doing in Wewoka. I don't know where he was killed. Or why. But there's one thing I do know. I want whoever killed him to stand trial for murder."

Cimarron rose. He dropped the empty envelope on the desk and pocketed the photograph. "I'll be on my way to Wewoka," he stated tonelessly. "It seems like the best place to start trying to find out who killed Cassidy. Be seeing you, Marshal."

Marshal Upham nodded and Cimarron turned and left the office.

2

Cimarron rode south along the east bank of Coon Creek toward Wewoka, thinking of Cassidy and silently damning whoever had killed him.

His right hand came to rest on the butt of his Frontier Colt .44. He looked down at the Winchester '73 in his saddle boot.

He rode on, the April sun hot on his broad shoulders and strong back, his lean hips swaying slightly with the motion of the bay beneath him. His long-fingered and heavily callused left hand gripped the horse's reins loosely as his long, lean legs guided the animal. He reached up and pulled his flat-topped black stetson down lower on his forehead to shadow his eyes and weatherworn face.

His cheeks were slightly sunken beneath his prominent cheekbones and they bordered a straight, flared-nostriled nose. His lips were thin and there were thinner lines at the edges of his emerald-green eyes. On his left cheek was a gray line of flesh that began just below his left eye, ran down along his cheek, and ended just above the corner of his mouth. The scar and the iciness of his eyes gave him a distinctly sinister look. His hair, broomstick-straight and as black as a moonless midnight, covered his ears and the nape of his neck.

His boots were dusty and worn down at the heels. His jeans were almost as dusty and badly faded. His black bib shirt showed signs of many washings as did his bandanna, once black but now faded to gray, that he wore tied loosely around the thick and corded column of his neck. The curled brim and crown of his sweat-stained stetson was also dusty and its black leather band showed signs of wear.

As the creek on his right widened, he used his knees to send a silent signal to the bay, and the animal angled to the left. He reached into his pocket and withdrew the deputy marshal's nickel badge he rarely wore. This time I want people to know what I am, he thought as he pinned the badge on his shirt. I want them to know I'm a lawman. I want them wary of me, maybe even afraid of me. A badge like mine's near as good as a gun with some people. It makes them skittish, and skittish folks aren't always so good at keeping secrets. They tend to talk too fast and too much and some-times to let secrets they wish they'd kept to themselves slip out. He rubbed the cuff of his shirt against the badge to polish it.

It caught the sun, glinted.

His left hand momentarily tightened on the reins when he heard the sudden and unexpected sound, but he did not draw rein.

Beaver, he thought as he recognized the sound.

The *slip-slap* of a beaver's tail on water, the animal's warning of danger in the vicinity, sounded again, and Cimarron glanced first to the left at the deep pool and then ahead of him at the beaver lodge that had dammed Coon Creek. The dam was a mound of branches, leaves, and mud that sprouted like an elongated mushroom from the water to span the width of the creek. He watched two small beavers slide smoothly—kind of giddily, he thought—down a slick mud slope and into the water. They were followed immediately by a full-grown beaver.

That one's their ma, he thought. She's been out looking after her kits, slapping the water to warn them that danger's coming their way, meaning me. Only she's wrong; I'm not dangerous. Not to those beavers down there under the water in their safe dry lodge. But to the killer, or killers, of

24

Cassidy? Now, that, he thought, is one whole other matter entirely. To whoever did for Cassidy, I fully intend being as dangerous as a teased sidewinder.

He rode on past the beaver lodge and, a little later, into the northern part of Wewoka. He found the main street easily and rode down it, reconnoitering the shops, the people on the street. The shops were standard: mercantile, tin shop, drugstore, lawyer's office, photographer's studio, livery stable, feed and grain store, sawmill, and some other miscellaneous establishments, including two restaurants and what he suspected was an illegal saloon. There was also a two-story, false-fronted hotel.

The people, by and large, ignored him. But some didn't. Some gave him the frankly appraising and sometimes uneasy looks townspeople give to strangers. He noticed that some of them, when they saw his badge gleaming in the sunlight, looked away into shop windows or straight ahead at nothing.

At the end of the street, beyond which lay grassland dotted with an occasional frame house, he turned the bay and rode back the way he had come. He drew rein in front of the building that was trying to hide its real nature by sporting a painted sign above its entrance that said piously and simply, SOCIAL CLUB.

He got out of the saddle, wrapped his bay's reins around the hitch rail, and shouldered his way through the batwings into a large square room. It was nearly empty, with four seated men and a man standing behind a counter that faced the door. He walked past the billiard and gaming tables, and when he reached the counter, he nodded to the man behind it.

"Nice morning," the man said as he drummed the fingers of one hand on the counter.

"No need for you to be nervous," Cimarron told him. "You've no doubt seen lawmen here in town before."

The drumming stopped. The man's lips pursed.

"You keep the ardent in the back room, do you?" The pursed lips of the man behind the counter split open, but before he could speak, Cimarron said, "I'm not here to arrest you. I'm here to have a drink. Whiskey."

The man's head swiveled silently from side to side.

"Are you trying to tell me something, mister?"

"No whiskey. This is a social club."

"Now, how the hell can you hope to run a social club without whiskey? Beer at least? I mean, just how social can a club like this one be without a taste or two of the ardent to lubricate the members' tongues and ease them into socializing with one another?"

"Selling the ardent in Indian Territory's against the law. And you're—" The man fell silent, as if the thought that had crossed his mind were causing him to pale. His eyes dropped to Cimarron's badge.

"And I'm the law." Cimarron leaned over the bar. "I'm also thirsty. I've rode all the way from Fort Smith with nothing to drink between there and here but the water of the Canadian and the water I got from Coon Creek a ways back."

"I'm a law-abiding citizen."

"You're a law-abiding citizen who's about to break the law on my orders. I won't tell if you won't."

The man looked to the right, to the left, and then back at Cimarron, who gestured at the door behind the counter. With obvious reluctance the man went through it. When he returned, he had a bottle of whiskey and a glass in his hands. He was about to pour some when he saw the photograph Cimarron had placed on the counter during his absence. He gasped and almost dropped the bottle and glass.

Cimarron reached out and took both from him. Silently, he filled his glass. Sipping from it, he stared at the man behind the counter, who was still looking, a horrified expression on his face, at the photograph.

"You ever seen him before?" Cimarron inquired between sips. "When he was alive? Or after he was dead?"

The man shook his head. He shuddered and looked up at Cimarron.

Cimarron sipped his whiskey, his eyes boring into those of the man across the counter from him. "He was a deputy marshal, same as me. I'm looking for whoever did that to him."

"How could anyone do a thing like that to another human being?" the man behind the counter murmured, still shaking his head. "It's . . . awful."

"I have to agree with you. It is that. But somebody could do it, and somebody went and did it. No polecat or possum did it. It was one or more two-legged critters or I miss my guess."

Cimarron turned to face the few men in the room. "Gents, I'd be obliged to you if you'd all step up here for a minute." When no one moved, Cimarron idly fingered his badge, looked down at it, spit on the cuff of his sleeve, and then rubbed the cuff on the badge.

His gesture seemed to spark new life in the four men seated facing him. All of them rose and hurried up to the counter.

Cimarron reached behind him, picked up the photograph, and held it out for the men to see. "What can you gents tell me about what you're looking at?"

"Nothing," one man said quickly before looking away from the photograph.

Another shook his head.

"He's a stranger to me," said a third.

The fourth asked, "What happened to him?"

"What happened to him?" Cimarron repeated incredulously. "You can see what happened to him. Somebody mistook him for Jesus Christ. What I want to know is where's the place that shows in that picture? Any of you recognize it?"

Four denials—swift, unequivocal.

"Any of you recognize the man in the picture?"

Four heads shook.

"None of you knows nothing about the man or what happened to him or who made it happen to him?"

"No, Marshal," said one of the men.

"Deputy marshal," Cimarron corrected him. "I may be in town awhile. Maybe I'll run into you gents again. Maybe when I do, one or more of you might remember something that escapes you at the moment."

27

Cimarron emptied his glass, tossed a coin on the counter, and strode out of the social club, pocketing the photograph as he went.

Outside, he halted and looked up and down the main street. His gaze came to rest on the hotel; his thoughts were of a soft bed with clean linen, but he shoved them aside, knowing that he might not be staying long in Wewoka. He knew he had only the slimmest of reasons for being in the town—the fact that the envelope containing the photograph of Cassidy had been mailed to Fort Smith from Wewoka. But that didn't mean, he told himself again, that Cassidy had been here or that he had been murdered here. It could have happened anywhere in the Territory, he thought with a sinking feeling. Somebody might have come upon Cassidy's corpse, took a picture of it, and then, when that somebody got to Wewoka, he could have sent the picture to Fort Smith.

Hold on, he advised himself. Not so damned fast. Why, he wondered, would anyone who might have taken the photograph in Seminole Nation, or even down in Chickasaw Nation, hold on to it until he got here to Wewoka before mailing it? And there was another matter bothering him. People didn't, as a rule, go riding around the Territory with a heavy camera and the equipment to go with it, although he'd once run into a man from *The New York Times* doing just that on the Comanche, Kiowa, and Apache reservation.

Photograph, he thought. Camera. His head turned and he stared at the sign above one of the shops he had passed earlier. Then he stepped down off the boardwalk and angled across the street, heading for the shop whose sign read, FAMILY PORTRAITS AND PHOTOGRAPHS TO COMMEMORATE ALL OCCASIONS.

When he reached it, he went inside and almost fell over a pasteboard figure of a cowboy wearing painted leather chaps and carrying a painted lasso. The figure had no head, Cimarron noticed as he steadied it to keep it from falling over.

"You don't need that photographic prop, sir," said a man who appeared from behind a black velvet curtain that hid the rear of the shop from sight. "You already look like a cowboy."

28

Cimarron went up to the man, who was smiling broadly, and said, "I've done my share of cowboying in my time, but at the moment I'm a deputy marshal."

The man's smile vanished. His upper lip twitched and the tiny brown mustache above it seemed to have a life of its own. "Is something wrong, Deputy? You're not here to have your portrait taken?"

"I'm not, and, yes, something's wrong." Cimarron pulled the photograph from his pocket and handed it to the man, whose mustache, as he looked down at it, leapt into new life.

"Oh, dear," the man said. "Oh, my."

"Did you take that picture?"

"No, oh, no. I'd never want to take a picture of—" He touched the photograph with the tip of his index finger. "Of that," he concluded softly, and handed the picture back to Cimarron.

"Have you any idea who might have taken it?"

"No. None."

"Do you know—can you tell me if it was taken near here?"

"I didn't recognize the locale, no."

"Have you ever seen the man in the picture?"

"Not to my knowledge, no." The man's hand smoothed his mustache as if he were trying to soothe it. "But I take it that you know the man."

"Like me, he's—he was a deputy marshal. His name's—it was Sean Cassidy." Cimarron realized that he was still having a hard time believing that Cassidy was dead. "He was also a good friend of mine."

"You're here to arrest whoever did that to him."

"I am, Mr.—"

"Bennett. Elmer Bennett. I own this studio. I'd be glad to be of service to you if you ever have the need of some lifelike likenesses of yourself, Deputy."

Cimarron nodded and left the studio. Once outside, he headed directly for the livery stable several doors down on the same side of the street. When he reached it, he spoke to the men lounging outside its open door. He told them who he was. He showed them the photograph. He asked questions and received negative answers to all of them.

But then a black man came out of the livery and Cimarron turned to him, identified himself, displayed the photograph, and asked him the same questions he had asked the others.

"That look like it might be out near Mr. August Child's place," the black man said, squinting at the photograph. "Mr. Child, he be a member of the Seminole tribal council. Got hisself a nice home, he do, with a whole lot of shin oaks growing around and about it. Trees just like the ones in this here picture."

One of the loungers laughed raucously. "Don't you pay no mind to Possum Jack, Deputy. His eyesight's about as good as my game leg. Besides which, shin oaks grow just about everywhere in Seminole Nation."

"That's right, Mr. Morton," Possum Jack said. "I guess I ought to get myself a pair of spectacles so's I can really see for sure what I'm looking at." Possum Jack looked from the loungers to Cimarron. "I'll be on my way, Mister Deputy. Sorry to see what some devil done to that poor soul."

When Possum Jack had gone, the man who had spoken earlier cleared his throat and said, "Don't put any store in what old Possum Jack Tucker tells you, Deputy. He's like any darky. Long on imagination, short on brains. He sees haunts everywhere."

Cimarron heard a noise from inside the livery and he went inside to find a stocky young man with wavy red hair trying to quiet a horse that was kicking the walls of its stall.

Cimarron went up to him and asked, "You work here, mister?"

"I own this livery. Name's Schuyler. Buster Schuyler. What can I do for you?"

Cimarron thrust the photograph at Schuyler. "What can you tell me about that?"

Schuyler looked at the photograph and then at the badge pinned to Cimarron's shirt. "Cassidy was a deputy too. He—"

"Buster!" one of the men shouted from the doorway.

30

"Get on out here so I can whup you at another game of checkers."

"I don't know anything about this," Schuyler told Cimarron and hastily returned the photograph. He hurried out of the livery, and when Cimarron came outside, he found Schuyler and another man seated on wooden crates, a checkerboard resting on another crate between them.

Pocketing the photograph, Cimarron strode down the street, thinking that he would talk to Schuyler some other time. Some other time when the man was alone. He was obviously afraid to talk, but just as obviously he had something to talk about. The checker player's summons had been, Cimarron believed, a way of silencing Schuyler.

He went into the hotel and up to the desk, where he registered and took the key with the numbered tag on it that the desk clerk handed him. As he mounted the steps to the second floor, he felt mild elation, because of Schuyler and what the man had said. He obviously knew something about Cassidy, and Cimarron made up his mind to find out just what Schuyler knew.

He unlocked the door to room number six and went inside, closing it behind him. He flopped down on his back on the lumpy bed and clasped his hands behind his head. Shin oaks, he thought. Possum Jack Tucker said that shin oaks grew around a Mr. August Child's place. I'll have to find out who and where this Child is. I'll have to have me another talk with Possum Jack, too, when the man's alone and not likely to be frightened off by some white son of a bitch who wants him to keep his mouth shut.

There was a soft knock on the door, and Cimarron, surprised, got up and went to it. "Who's out there?" he barked, his hand on the butt of his .44.

"Let me in!"

A man's voice. Faintly familiar. Not Possum Jack, though. Cimarron opened the door to find Schuyler standing outside in the hall.

The owner of the livery scurried past Cimarron and into the

room. "Close the door. Close it quick before somebody sees me in here."

Cimarron closed the door and stood staring at Schuyler—at the man's stocky body, which was on the verge of becoming fat, at his nearly chinless face. Then he asked, "You got something you want to say to me?"

"They're all afraid. That's why they wouldn't answer your questions. And if you ask me, maybe one or more of them doesn't want the truth known—not by a lawman like you. I watched where you went after you left the livery, and first chance I got, I came here and the desk clerk told me what room you were in."

"Why'd you come here, Schuyler?"

"To warn you."

"Warn me about what?"

"That you might wind up the same way that other deputy did if the vigilantes take a notion that you're here to make trouble for them."

"Vigilantes?"

"They're the ones who killed Cassidy. There's a lot of them in and around Wewoka, but nobody knows how many exactly or who they are. Or if they do know, they sure enough aren't saying. They figure if they keep their mouths shut and their noses clean, the vigilantes won't come after *them*."

"Why'd these vigilantes kill Cassidy?"

"Because of Jimmy Jumper—him and Clementine Jordan. Eunice Jordan, too. And because of what Roley Jumper did."

"Take yourself a seat, Schuyler," Cimarron said, pointing to a wooden chair near the bed. "Then get your breath and say what you've got to say to me, only say it slow. I can't follow you past the first fence post the way you're talking so fast at me."

Schuyler sat down, and after Cimarron had seated himself on the bed, the liveryman said, "Jimmy Jumper—he's a young Seminole—was paying court to Eunice Jordan, though she's only seventeen and him not but two or so years older. This younger generation is—"

"Schuyler." When Cimarron had the man's attention, he said, "Start at the beginning and speak your piece. Leave out the moralizing and stop traveling trails that don't lead anywhere worth going."

"I guess Jimmy got tired of Eunice and interested in her mother, Clementine. Mrs. Jordan was a good-looking woman, that's for sure. Anyway, he raped her and then he strangled her. He left her body lying out in the front yard and wild hogs came out of the woods and ate some of it before Eunice came out of hiding in the barn where she'd run to get away from Jimmy after what he'd done to her mother."

"Eunice Jordan saw this fellow, Jimmy Jumper, rape and kill her ma?"

Schuyler nodded. "When she told her pa what Jimmy had done, Clay Jordan was fit to be tied, I can tell you. Well, word spread fast, the way it does in small towns like Wewoka. First thing anybody knew the word was out from the vigilantes that Jimmy Jumper's life wasn't worth a hole in a boot sole. They were going to get him, they said. When Roley Jumper—that's Jimmy's father—heard that, he got real scared. He knew what the vigilantes were capable of doing to men who'd done what Jimmy had done. So he rushed right out and collared Deputy Cassidy, who'd come to town the day before to see a lady, although not everyone in town would call Mae Holloway a lady because of the way she—"

"Schuyler!"

"Where was I? Oh, yes. So Roley went to Cassidy and asked him to take Jimmy into protective custody to save him from the vigilantes and their brand of justice. Cassidy did. But the vigilantes—they seem to know every move everybody in town makes before they even make it—they bushwhacked Cassidy and Jimmy outside of town.

"Jimmy got away from them, but they got Cassidy. I guess the fact of Jimmy slipping through their fingers made them mad. Anyway, they crucified Cassidy for going against them."

"That's what he died of—those nails they drove into him? Loss of blood?"

Schuyler shook his head. "They let him hang there for a

33

spell and then one of the vigilantes put a bullet in his back. It never came out of the front of him. It must have hit a rib or something.''

"How come you know all this?"

"I was coming home that night from delivering a horse to one of my customers out past August Child's place, which is due west of where Cassidy was killed. I saw some lights flickering in the distance. At first, I thought they were coming from August Child's. But they were torches.

"I got out of the saddle and hid in a grove of shin oaks. I watched them crucify Cassidy. It was some sight, let me tell you, that one was!''

"Did you recognize any of the vigilantes?"

"How could I? Oh, I guess I forgot to mention that they wear hoods as black as the robes they also wear so nobody can see who they are. The hoods have eyeholes in them so they can see and nose holes so they can breathe.''

Cimarron leaned forward and rested his forearms on his knees, his hands clasped. "What if it wasn't Jimmy Jumper who raped and murdered Mrs. Jordan?"

"It was. Eunice saw him do it.''

"These vigilantes," Cimarron said after a moment, "don't strike me as the kind of men I'd want to mix with.''

"I know just exactly what you mean, Deputy. Everybody's afraid of them, and with damned good reason, too.''

"That's not what I meant. What I meant was, I wouldn't want to have anything to do with a pack of men who could do what they did to Cassidy." Cimarron got up, went to the window, and looked out. "Where's Jimmy Jumper now?"

"Nobody knows.''

"Not even the vigilantes?"

"If they knew, they'd have done for him by now.''

"I came out here to find Cassidy—and to find out what happened to him. Looks like I've got more than those matters to handle.''

"You mean the murder of Mrs. Jordan.''

"I do. Schuyler, can you show me the spot where they

killed Cassidy?'' Cimarron turned from the window. ''Is his body still there?''

''Far as I know, it is. Sure, I can show you the spot. But are you real sure you want to see it—him, if he's still tacked up to those planks out there?''

Cimarron nodded.

''I'll get my horse and meet you outside of town—the north side. It wouldn't do for me to be seen with you. I guess you can understand that, Deputy.''

Cimarron nodded again and then both men left the hotel room.

Schuyler led Cimarron through a pass and into a valley that was surrounded by low-lying hills and whose floor was covered with a dense growth of shin oaks. As the two men rode through the trees, Schuyler glanced nervously over his shoulder, just as he had been doing throughout the ride from Wewoka.

''This is the place?'' Cimarron asked him.

''There's a clearing up ahead.''

When they reached it, Cimarron, ignoring Schuyler's warning to stay under the cover of the trees, rode up to the scene of the crude crucifixion. He drew rein and stood staring at the naked body of Cassidy. The buzzards had plucked out his eyes and his entrails, and the ground animals had gnawed his feet and his legs down to the bone.

Cimarron noticed the dried blood staining the bluebells that were nodding in the breeze beside Cassidy's feet.

''It was an awful way to die,'' Schuyler said as he rode up beside Cimarron. ''I watched them pound those nails into his hands and feet. I can still hear the sound of the hammer. I can still hear his screams.''

''I'll get the ones who did this if I—''

''The blood spurted out,'' Schuyler said in a distant voice, interrupting Cimarron. ''All over it went. Even as loud as the hammer was on the nails, you could still hear the sounds of his bones splintering when the nails smashed into them.''

Cimarron glanced covertly at Schuyler and saw the faraway,

almost dreamy look on the man's face as he sat his saddle and stared down at what was left of Cassidy.

"Those butchers were worse than the Plains Indians," Schuyler commented. "Imagine what it must have been like for that deputy—the pain, it must have been unbearable. And the blood, you can see where it ran down his arms. It's all dried up now, but at the time it was as bright as new red ribbons."

Cimarron's eyes remained on Schuyler's face and something about the man's rapt expression and the way he spoke bothered him, but at the same time they reminded him of something. Only when Schuyler began describing how Cassidy had begged the vigilantes to shoot him to end his agony, did Cimarron realize what he had been reminded of. Himself. The way he sometimes spoke to a woman, soft and sensuously, after she had let him love her.

But there was an undertone to Schuyler's voice, too, and Cimarron recognized it as one of excitement as Schuyler talked on, recreating for himself the spectacle of Cassidy's crucifixion and eventual execution.

"He didn't die right away, even after they shot him," Schuyler said with an odd eagerness coloring his tone. "He hung on awhile. He talked. I couldn't hear what he was saying or trying to say from where I was hiding back there in the trees because he was mumbling by that time. But he must have been begging for another bullet because I did hear one of the men say, 'One's all you're going to get.' Then they all rode away."

"Did you?"

"Not right away."

"Did you try to help him?"

Schuyler, his eyes still on Cassidy's corpse, shook his head. "There was nothing I could do at that point. He was too far gone."

Cimarron got out of the saddle.

"What are you going to do?"

He didn't answer Schuyler as he pulled his bowie knife

from his right boot and began to pry out the nails that pinioned Cassidy's body to the two crossed planks.

Later, as he placed his friend's corpse over the neck of his bay, the horse shivered and then blew because it had smelled blood.

Schuyler asked, "What are you going to do with him?"

"Take him into town and arrange to have him buried."

"Doing that's like flaunting yourself right in the face of the vigilantes," Schuyler warned ominously.

"It's got to be done, and done decent," Cimarron responded as he swung into the saddle. He turned the bay toward the trees and headed for them.

3

Cimarron left the mortician's after making arrangements for the burial of Cassidy's body in the Seminole cemetery outside of Wewoka. He made his way to the home of Mae Holloway, following the directions Schuyler had given him before they had parted.

He had no trouble finding the house, which was on one of the side streets that intersected the main one. A trellis, painted white and with a wisteria vine climbing it, rose from the ground in front of the porch. Cimarron got out of the saddle, and leaving his bay tethered to the white picket fence, he went through the gate, across the yard, and up on the porch. The front door was open. He knocked on the screen door.

"Come in," a woman's voice called out cheerfully from the rear of the house.

Cimarron went inside the hall and then hesitated. "Miss Holloway," he called out.

A woman with wisps of ash-blond hair falling down over her forehead, appeared at the other end of the hall. When she saw Cimarron, she nodded a wordless greeting. She was well-built, Cimarron noted, with wide hips below a narrow waist. Above her waist, her plump breasts strained against the checkered calico confining them as if they were eager to be free of their cloth prison. Her eyes were large and luminous beneath sharply arched eyebrows—a gray that was almost blue. There was a dimple in her chin, and above it her lips were bowed and provocatively full.

She brushed the hair from her forehead with a languid hand that was white with flour. Her voice, when she spoke to Cimarron, was pleasantly light and lilting. "I don't believe I know you, do I?"

"No, Miss Holloway, you don't. But I'm a deputy marshal and I heard about you, so I came here to—"

"Come into the kitchen. I've been baking."

Cimarron followed her into the kitchen and she pointed to a chair. He sat down in it as Mae Holloway plunged her arms almost all the way up to the elbows in a mass of springy dough that rested on a wooden bread board. "You look like the kind of man I wouldn't mind knowing. I have a weakness for lawmen."

"That's what I came here to talk to you about, Miss Holloway. A lawman. Sean Cassidy."

"Call me Mae, Deputy."

"I was wondering if you knew anything about what happened to Cassidy."

Mae picked up a tin sifter and sprinkled flour over the dough she had been kneading. "I know he's dead, if that's what you mean. I know he was killed—crucified by the vigilantes."

"I know that much myself," Cimarron said. "I thought you might be able to tell me something about these Wewoka vigilantes. Who they are. How many of them there are."

"What's your name, Deputy?"

"Cimarron."

"Well, Cimarron, I can't help you there." Mae placed the dough in a greased pan and placed it inside the oven. "Nobody knows who they are," she added as she carefully closed the oven door. "And I, for one, don't want to know."

"I, for one, *do* want to know who they are, all of them."

"You're going to arrest them?"

"For murder. Yes."

Mae threw back her head and laughed. Then she sat down

across from Cimarron. "You're one man. They're a whole bunch."

"That's true."

"They'll skin you alive."

"Not if I can help it, they won't."

"Sean told me he wasn't afraid of them either when he was here." Mae looked down at the floury bread board in front of her. "He should have been. I told him he should have been. But— Did you know Sean?" When Cimarron nodded, she continued, "Then you know there was no use trying to guide that bullheaded Irishman any more than there's any use in trying to stop the sun from shining on a clear day. He wouldn't be pushed and he wouldn't be led. I told him he should leave Wewoka with Jimmy Jumper. Right away, I told him he should leave. But he wouldn't."

"Why? He had business here in town to take care of?"

Mae looked up at Cimarron and smiled shyly. "He had me to take care of." She folded her hands on the table in front of her, and Cimarron watched the two fat tears form in her eyes and then spill over her lower lids to slide down her cheeks. "It's my fault that he's dead."

"Mae, it's not."

"It is," she cried, slamming one hand down on the table and causing the bread board to bounce. "I should have *made* him leave with Jimmy . . . But the truth is, I really didn't want him to go. We hadn't seen each other in months. I was so glad when he showed up here that day that I could have danced a jig for joy."

"Cassidy was a man who made up his own mind, as you said before, Mae. You can't—you shouldn't—blame yourself for what happened to him.

"But I *do*!"

Mae's tears came in earnest this time, and as she wept, her tears made dark damp spots on the flour-powdered board.

Cimarron remained silent, watching her as her grief assaulted and then overwhelmed her. "I know how you feel, Mae," he said several minutes later when her sobs had subsided somewhat. "Cassidy was a good man."

Mae looked up at him. "A good man? Cimarron, he was one of the best." She sniffed and then managed a provocative smile. "In more ways than one, I can tell you."

Cimarron, remembering Cassidy and the man's easy way with women, nodded. He almost smiled back at Mae but didn't, fearing that his smile might be misinterpreted.

"Well, he's dead now," she stated bluntly, tossing her head in an angry gesture. "Life goes on; has to, I guess. At least, that's what people say. But I'll miss him. Oh, I will miss him."

"You sound like you got good memories of him to cherish."

"I do. Sean Cassidy was a high-living, hell-defying kind of man that made a woman like me realize that life was well worth living. Why, when he'd take me out to the Social Club here in town of a night, I never needed whiskey to lift my spirits. Sean lifted them for me. Remember how he used to laugh? How his laugh would start deep down in his throat and come rumbling up and spill out of his mouth as loud and soul-stirring as any bible-thumper's bombast?"

Cimarron remembered. "He was a man who could woo almost any woman, I'd wager, with his wicked words and devilish blue eyes."

Mae sighed. "Ah, yes, he was. He most certainly was. When I was with Sean Cassidy, I knew not only that life was worth living but also that, having known him, I could lie down and die happy and not ask for any other man to ever come courting me. Not that any of them in this town would. Not likely! To them, I'm not the kind of woman you court. To them, I'm the kind of woman you use and then walk away from. That is, until the need starts them itching again and they come slinking up to my back door, trying to pretend to themselves that it'll be just one last time and then they'll stay safe at home with their wives and children. Then Mae Holloway will be a dream—no, a nightmare—they'll forget they ever had."

Mae got up and went to the sink. She began washing the flour from her hands. "You said you'd heard about me, Cimarron."

"I was told that you were a friend of Cassidy's."

She turned, hands on hips, to face him. "That's all?"

He nodded.

"Sean was only one of the men I—knew. There are a goodly number of them here in Wewoka who come to call on me—if not to pay their respects to me exactly."

"Some of your gentlemen friends—could they be vigilantes?"

"I've no way of knowing. If they are, you can be sure they're not going to let me in on their little secret. Those vigilantes are a tightly spun bunch. I'd say the odds are that some of my gentlemen callers are probably in on it. Maybe that's why the vigilantes never made any trouble for me. If they ever do—" Mae came to the table, picked up a floury wooden rolling pin, and brandished it over Cimarron's head.

He cowered in mock fear before her.

"I'm not afraid of them," she insisted. "But Jimmy Jumper, I expect he is, and with good reason. You heard about the murder?"

"I was told that a woman named Clementine Jordan was raped and murdered and that her daughter claims she saw Jimmy Jumper commit the crimes."

Mae sat down at the table and sighed. "Sean was trying to protect Jimmy from the vigilantes. Now he's dead and Jimmy's on the run, and Jimmy had better run fast and far, if you ask me."

"Do you think Jimmy's guilty?"

Mae shrugged. "Hot blood—in men or women—can boil over, and then there's usually hell to pay."

"Do you think Jimmy is guilty?" Cimarron asked again.

"He could be. Clementine Jordan was a good-looking woman and Jimmy Jumper's young and he's not blind."

"I was told Jimmy was paying court to Eunice Jordan."

"He was. But does that mean he wouldn't harbor a yearning for a woman as full-figured and fair-faced as Clementine Jordan was?"

"Was Mrs. Jordan the kind of woman to lead a man down the primrose path?"

"Not that one," Mae declared forcefully. "Very prim and

42

twice as proper she was where men other than her husband, Clay, were concerned.''

''I've known women—men, too—who were the first to church on Sundays and the last to leave after the service, but they spent the other six days steeped in sin.''

Mae laughed, a throaty sound. ''People like that give me a pain in the butt. Sanctimonious as a circuit-riding preacher, and down underneath—and not so *far* down underneath neither—they're rutting right along with the rest of us folks they treat as inferiors. It's kind of funny and it's also kind of sad, seems to me.''

''Must take a lot of hard work keeping their two lives separate.''

''I expect so. But I've never had that problem. Me, I guess I'm either too stupid or too lazy to be anything other than just what I am.''

''You're a real nice lady, Mae.''

''Lady? Me? Cimarron, you are a hoot! A lady doesn't go around bestowing her favors as free as I've done over the years. There's another name for a female who does that.''

Cimarron said nothing.

''You're not wet behind the ears, Deputy. I bet you knew about me the minute you laid eyes on me. Before I told you a thing.''

''Mae, if you're trying to make me fit the mold of some of the hypocritical people you've run into in your life, you're bound to fail, on account of I don't go around calling people names and I don't go around pasting labels on them.''

Mae met Cimarron's steady gaze and held it for a long moment. ''You remind me of—'' She fell silent.

''Of Cassidy?''

She nodded mutely.

Cimarron rose. ''You'll find somebody else, Mae.''

''I already have.''

''There you go! I knew you would.''

Mae got up from the table. She took a step toward Cimarron, then another, until she was standing very close to him.

''Mae, you don't mean—''

43

"I do. I know it's awful of me. After what I just told you about Sean and me—about the way I felt about him. But it's just that now that he's gone and won't ever come to me again—there's a need in me, Cimarron. Night and day there's this gnawing need. I suppose I should try to snuff it out, drown it, do something about it. But I don't seem ever to be able to. In fact, I don't even try anymore. When a man—a long-limbed and hard-bodied man like you—comes near me, I feel a flutter inside me somewhere and I hear a voice saying, 'Mae, just imagine what it would be like to snuggle up close to a stud like that.' I know it's shameful. But you're a man who can arouse a woman with one quick look out of those green eyes of yours, whether you know it or not. And the way you move—like an animal on the prowl. Even your voice—it's like the sound of distant thunder in August that makes critters flit and shudder because they can feel the storm coming . . ."

Mae took another step, and as her body touched Cimarron's, his arms went around her. He bent his head as she raised hers and their lips met. Mae's mouth opened and Cimarron's tongue slid into it. He probed, his tongue darting, circling, Mae's touching it, teasing it.

Her hands came to rest on his shoulders and then they slid down his upper arms. They gripped his hips, flowed down his thighs and then up them again. She moved her body slightly, sucking his tongue now, so that her hands could glide between their bodies and come to rest on his groin, where she cupped his testicles in one hand and squeezed his throbbing erection with the other.

Their lips parted and Mae exclaimed, "And I thought I'd never meet a man who had a bigger poker than a cowboy I once knew up in Salinas. He was a marvel, but, Cimarron, you're— It's a *miracle*!" She hugged him, giggled, took his hand, "Let's go upstairs."

He let her hurry him up the stairs to the second floor and into her bedroom, which was a lush wonderland of white lace and red velvet. There were white lace curtains covering the windows, and white lace, in an elaborate design, edged the red velvet bedspread. The same white lace fringed the red velvet pillows on the chairs and on the window seat. A lace runner covered the top of the dresser and crushed red velvet framed the mirror above it.

"Don't stand on ceremony," she told him as she unbuttoned and slipped out of her dress.

Watching her slither out of her undergarments, Cimarron unbuckled his cartridge belt and let it drop to the floor. As Mae kicked off her shoes and bent down to roll down her stockings, he tossed his hat on a chair, untied his bandanna and sent it whirling after his hat, pulled his shirt over his head, dropped it . . .

She was in front of him and undoing the buttons of his jeans before he could reach for them. He let her ease his jeans down and then, at her urging, sat down on the bed and let her pull off his boots and then his jeans.

He reached up and placed his hands on her breasts. He squeezed her nipples and then leaned forward and licked them, one by one, as she stood with her hands on his shoulders, looking down at him.

She sighed and he looked up at her, at the lust rampant in her eyes, at her slightly parted lips. She drew his head close to her body. His left cheek was pressed against the warm flat plain of her belly and his left hand covered her mound. She moaned slightly as he thrust his middle finger into her and then moved it slowly in and out, in and out.

She withdrew from him, lay down upon the bed, and drew him down beside her. He started to turn toward her, intending to cover her, eager to enter her and ease his own lust, when she slid away from him. Then she was up and squatting above his loins as he lay on his back, looking up at her and wondering what she had in mind.

He found out.

Mae planted her feet firmly beside his hips, her knees bent and the palms of her hands resting on his chest. She swiveled her pelvis into position above his erection, and he raised his head and saw himself begin to disappear within her.

"Ah, now, that does feel fine, honey," he murmured as

her fingers teased his nipples into stiff attention and her pelvis sank until he was all the way within her.

She raised her pelvis and he looked down at the base of his shaft, wet with her juices. Then he looked up at her. Her eyes were closed, her neck arched, and her head thrown back as she slowly pistoned him, causing his head to snap back against the pillow and his toes to twist as ecstasy seized and shook him, causing his body to shudder.

"Now," she whispered, "like this." And she was suddenly flat on her back on the soft bed. She raised her legs until her feet were beside her head.

Cimarron got up on his knees facing her, and looking down and gripping his shaft with his right hand to guide it, he started to enter her. But she removed his hand, stroked him deftly twice, and then, holding him tightly, eased him into her. He was supporting himself with his hands flat on the bed, and as his hips slapped against her, her fingers teased his nipples.

And then Mae stretched her legs out and pulled him down upon her and his body bucked as he felt himself exploding within her and felt her erupt under him. Pleasure flooded throughout his entire body.

Mae's legs rose to wrap themselves around his thighs. He lay on her, still bucking as a result of his orgasm, his head buried against her neck, his nostrils breathing in the scent of lemon verbena that seemed to envelope her entire body.

He felt her fingers burrowing through his hair. He felt one of her hands on his neck and then the other one trace the trail of his spine down to where it ended just above his buttocks. He sighed, awash in a sea of pleasure as she kissed his cheeks, his nose, his lips. He sighed again as she nuzzled his right earlobe.

He let himself ride the sweet tide of her scent for a time he could not measure, and he wasn't sure just when they separated and lay there side by side, all his senses sated.

"So good," he heard her murmur.

"It was," he agreed, and moved closer to her warm and softly scented body.

Silence then, as they touched each other gently, almost shyly, after the boldness of their just-ended encounter.

He raised his head and kissed her. "I swore I'd get the men who murdered Cassidy because he was my friend. Because of the way they killed him. Now I've got me one more reason."

Mae waited for him to go on.

"They took his life from him and, in the taking, they stole you from him along with the sun and clouds, the good times and the bad. That's a crime, Mae. One they'll pay for, and pay dear."

Mae's hands rose and cupped his face. "I hope you get them, Cimarron. For Sean's sake. For mine."

"I'll get them. You can count on it."

The next morning, as the sun threw golden spears through the windows of his hotel room, Cimarron groaned in his sleep as he felt himself fleeing in desperation through the dark streets and alleys of his anguished dream from the dead man who relentlessly pursued him.

He turned corners. He doubled back. He hid in dim doorways.

The man could not be eluded. He came on, his feet methodically pounding the earth, thudding threateningly in Cimarron's mind. Tears streamed from the man's empty eyes as he pursued his son, and Cimarron, running for his life and his sanity, covered his ears as the dead man—the father he had murdered—called out to him to stop, to explain.

The dreamscape shifted. Mist swirled through it. Cimarron was once again in the bank in the Texas Panhandle, and he was once again, in his dream, reliving the moments before he would fire the shot that would shatter his life and make him a secretly haunted man.

Kneeling in front of the iron safe and scooping paper money in neatly bound bundles into a cloth sack, he had his back to the door of the bank he was robbing along with his confederates. Behind him, on the other side of the tellers'

47

barred stations, the petrified patrons of the bank stood with raised hands and alarmed eyes.

A shout—a warning.

Cimarron turned. He saw the figure of the lawman silhouetted in the doorway, and he unleathered his revolver and fired. As the man he had hit crumpled, Cimarron was up and running along with the other outlaws, past the gaping patrons, past the dead sheriff lying faceup on the wooden floor.

He skidded to a sudden halt. Turned. Looked down. His world tilted and then rocked violently.

He shouted questions, and the men and women in the bank, their trembling hands still raised, answered them.

The sheriff—a good man—had come to their town—after his wife had died—they had elected him their sheriff . . .

Cimarron looked down again, frozen because of the ice that now flowed in his veins and then he was running from the bank and tossing the sack full of money to one of the other outlaws. He was astride his horse and riding hard— away from the bank, away from the men with whom he had been riding, away from himself and the awful fact that the sheriff he had killed had been the man who had fathered him in a long-ago and happier time.

But the sheriff, his slaughtered father, had followed him.

He had followed him through the canyons and across the mesas of his mind in the years that followed, and he had called out time and time again to his son, asking him to explain what he had done, tears drier than dust oozing from his dead eyes.

Cimarron's body lurched and stiffened in the bed. His eyes snapped open. He sat up, cold sweat running from every pore of his naked body. He squeezed his eyes shut and clenched his fists, longing for freedom from the ghost that would not be denied, the ghost that ambushed him at every opportunity and taught him that his present was, in part, the anguished product of his unalterable past.

He lay down on his back, and as he did so, he became aware that his fists were clenched tightly at his sides. He opened them and lay still, his eyes still closed, listening to the wild thumping of his heart and trying hard not to understand the message it was sending him.

Someone knocked on the door.

He sprang from the bed and stood, legs spread, beside it. "Who's out there?"

"Roley Jumper. I have to talk to you."

Jimmy Jumper's father, Cimarron thought as he reached for his jeans. He hurriedly pulled them and his boots on. He then crossed the room, unlocked and opened the door.

"Cimarron?" inquired the sober-faced man standing in the hall. He had flat features, except for his aquiline nose. His black eyes were round and his equally black hair was as straight as Cimarron's own. His skin was the color of old hickory and there were deeply embedded lines on his broad forehead.

"I'm Cimarron."

"May I come in?"

Cimarron stepped aside and the other man entered the room. As Cimarron closed the door, Jumper turned and said, "I've come to talk to you about my son."

"Go ahead and talk, Mr. Jumper. I'll listen."

"I learned of your presence in town late yesterday," Jumper said as he sat down in the chair by the window. "I came to tell you that there are men in this town who are trying to kill Jimmy, my son."

"Vigilantes," Cimarron said as he put on his shirt and then tied his bandanna around his neck.

"So you know about them. Good. Then you know my son's life is in grave danger. You do, that is, if you've heard about the murder of Mrs. Jordan."

"I've heard about it. People say your son killed Mrs. Jordan."

"They're wrong. He didn't. Jimmy is not a killer."

"There was, I'm told, an eyewitness."

"Eunice Jordan is lying."

"How do you happen to know that?"

"I just know it. I can't prove it, but I know Jimmy and I know he would never kill anyone. He's a good boy, although

49

I'm willing to admit he has a sharp edge to his temper at times. He has been employed as a bookkeeper by the tribal council for nearly a year now. He's a solid, responsible citizen of Seminole Nation. He has never been in any kind of trouble before.''

"Mr. Jumper, there turns out to be a first time for just about anything under the sun that a man might care to name. Including rape and murder, in your son's case.''

"If you don't believe my judgment concerning my son, I urge you to talk to August Child. He's a senior member of the tribal council and he knows Jimmy well. In fact, he was the one who hired Jimmy.''

"What kind of bookkeeping did your son do, Mr. Jumper?''

"He kept track of the tribe's cash flow. Annuity payments received from the federal government. Disbursements made by the tribe to discharge its legal obligations. He held a very responsible job, as I've said. It was not the sort of occupation for a man capable of rape or murder.''

"A man never knows when he gets up in the morning what he's going to be capable of before he lays himself back down again at night, Mr. Jumper.''

"That is, I must say, a most cynical attitude you have, Cimarron.''

"Not cynical. Practical. It's based on observations I've made and experiences I've had. Why would Eunice Jordan want to lie about your son?''

Jumper shook his head sadly. "I've no idea . . . none. She and Jimmy—he'd been courting Eunice for nearly a year. I know that did not set well with her father. Clay Jordan, like many other whites here in the Nation, has his prejudices against Indians. Many whites resent the fact that we Seminoles have our own tribal laws and government. They dislike our custom of holding land in common among the members of our tribe. Most of all, I believe, they deeply resent the fact that we Seminoles receive annuity payments from the United States government—*their* government, as they perceive it. Then, too, there is the matter—important to many whites in the Nation—that we are not, as they are, descendants of white European stock."

"Are you telling me that whites—white vigilantes—want to raise hell with your son because they're bigots?"

"I am suggesting that racial prejudice may indeed play a part in this matter. So, too, might the fact that there has been bad blood between myself and Clay Jordan for some time now."

"How come?"

"Jordan leases land from me. For nearly a year now, he has failed to make the payments due me for the right to lease that land. I have tried and failed to collect what is rightfully due me. Jordan has retaliated by forbidding his daughter to see my son."

"How'd Jimmy take that?"

"He was, naturally enough, angered. He and Eunice, however, continued to meet each other secretly. I tell you, Cimarron, Jimmy had no reason, no motive, to murder Mrs. Jordan."

"Well, I can tell you, Mr. Jumper, that I plan on looking into this matter of Mrs. Jordan's murder. By the way, do you happen to know where your son is at the moment?"

"No, I do not. When the vigilantes attacked him and Deputy Cassidy and Jimmy escaped from them, he came to me and told me he was going to have to hide until the real murderer of Mrs. Jordan was apprehended. I haven't seen or heard from him since."

"I've been told that Deputy Cassidy had taken your son under his wing to keep the vigilantes from getting their hands on him."

"That's correct. He did so at my request. You know what happened to Cassidy?"

"I know. That's what brought me here." Cimarron pulled the photograph of Cassidy from his pocket and handed it to Jumper. "Did you send this to Fort Smith?"

"No. You don't know who did?"

Cimarron shook his head. "Somebody, it seems, wanted the law to know what had happened to Cassidy."

"Why?"

"Maybe it was an act of good citizenship on somebody's part. Or maybe somebody wanted justice done, and I don't mean vigilante justice."

"Cimarron, I came here today to ask you to find Jimmy and to protect him. Take him back to Fort Smith with you and jail him there if you must. Put him on trial in Judge Parker's court. I am confident that he will be found innocent of the crimes Eunice Jordan has accused him of committing."

Jumper reached into his pocket and withdrew a small leather purse. "I am fully prepared to pay you for your trouble."

"No need to do that, Jumper." Cimarron went to the window and stood staring down into the street. "I've had it in mind to do what you've just asked me to do. Not take your boy into protective custody exactly, though that might wind up being what I'll have to do. He's an Indian. Mrs. Jordan was a white woman. Judge Parker's court's got jurisdiction when an Indian here in the Territory is accused of committing a crime against a white man or woman, as you most likely know. So arresting your boy's my job. Just as it's my job to bring in whoever it was crucified Deputy Cassidy."

"You won't hurt him?"

Cimarron turned from the window to face Jumper. "I will if he tries to hurt me."

Jumper, looking crestfallen, got to his feet.

"What's your boy look like, Jumper? What was he wearing when you last saw him? Who are his friends? What are his habits?"

When Jumper had answered Cimarron's questions, he added, "My wife has been dead for several years now, Cimarron. Jimmy is all I have left. He was the only child Bettina and I had."

"I appreciate that fact, Jumper. But, then, Mrs. Jordan was the only wife Clay Jordan had and the only mother Eunice Jordan had."

Jumper tried and failed to meet the stony stare Cimarron was giving him. He turned and left the room, his shoulders slumping, a disconsolate expression on his troubled face.

4

As Cimarron bent over to tighten the cinch strap on his bay, Buster Schuyler, standing just outside the stall that housed the bay, commented, "It's none of my business, Deputy, but it seems to me you'd do a whole lot better were you to try to catch that Injun instead of wasting time talking to Clay Jordan."

Cimarron straightened and flipped down his stirrups. "I'm obliged to you, Schuyler, for giving me directions to the Jordan place."

"That Jimmy Jumper's a menace to civilized society," Schuyler remarked, stroking his almost nonexistent chin. "I do wish either you or the vigilantes would catch up with him before he decides to go on another murdering rampage."

Cimarron led the bay out of the stall and then out of the livery.

Schuyler followed him outside, and as Cimarron swung into the saddle, he said, "I heard tell that Jimmy's pa was over to the hotel to see you this morning."

"News sure travels fast here in Wewoka."

"Did he?"

"Did who what?" Cimarron asked, deliberately stalling.

"Did Roley Jumper pay you a visit?" When Cimarron nodded, Schuyler asked, "What did he want, if you don't mind my asking?"

"He wanted me to take over where Cassidy left off."

Schuyler, frowning, scratched his head. After a minute, he said, "Oh, I guess I get it. He wants you to take care of his boy." When Cimarron nodded again, Schuyler, as he idly stroked the nose of the bay, said, "Deputy, you're either a very brave or a very foolish man. When the vigilantes hear you're taking it upon yourself to coddle Jimmy—and they will hear of it, don't you doubt that—you'll find real trouble traveling the trail right behind you. You ride careful now, you hear?"

Cimarron heeled the bay and rode north through the town and then out of it. When he came to Wewoka Creek just beyond the northern border of the town, he turned the bay to the left and rode along the southern bank until he came to the cultivated ground that, Schuyler had told him, was leased by Clay Jordan from Roley Jumper. In the distance was a solitary figure. The man, his hands on the handles of a plow, was bent over as he followed behind the large quarter horse.

Remembering the description Schuyler had given him, Cimarron recognized the man in the field as Clay Jordan. He got out of the saddle and wrapped the reins around a low-hanging branch of a chokecherry tree. He strode into the field and made his way up to Jordan.

The man, Cimarron observed, was tall, thin, and bony, with huge hands and a hard-bitten expression on his face. His eyes, as he glanced questioningly at Cimarron, were dark-brown and wary. He straightened, and as he did so, Cimarron half-expected to hear his bones creak and snap. Jordan took off his straw hat, pulled a handkerchief from his pocket, and wiped the sweat from his face and almost entirely bald head.

" 'Morning, Jordan. My name's Cimarron. I'm a—"

"Know who you are."

"You do?"

"Some friends of mine told me all about you, Deputy. Know that you came to town yesterday, that you're looking for the killers of that other deputy, that interfering son of a bitch named Cassidy."

"I also happen to be on the scout for the man who raped and murdered your wife."

"Then why the hell ain't you out after Jimmy Jumper instead of standing in the middle of my field wasting your time and mine, too?"

"I wanted to have a talk with you about what happened to your wife, Jordan. I also want to talk to Eunice about the same thing."

"He left my wife out in the yard. The chickens pecked out her eyes, both of them. The hogs—wild ones that roam the woods down there—came out and ate parts of her. If I'd been home—"

"You weren't home when the crimes were committed?"

"I was up north in Coonsville on business. If I'd have been to home, that Jumper fellow would never have had the chance to lay so much as a finger on my Clementine." Jordan swore. He put his hat back on, pocketed his handkerchief, and stared out across his field. "We were married for nineteen years, Clementine and me. Nineteen good years. And during all that time I never could get myself used to the idea that a good-looking woman like Clementine would give me so much as the time of day, let alone her hand in holy matrimony.

"I miss her something fierce, and that's a fact. She was what lighted up my life. Now it's all dark all the time. You married, Deputy?"

Cimarron shook his head.

"Then you don't know what it's like living close to somebody day in and day out, come sunshine or storm, good times or bad. Feeling her next to you in bed at night. Seeing her in the house or the fields and knowing she's yours and you're hers, and having a daughter that's part her and part you, and being fool enough to believe it would all go on like that forever and ever without no end. But nothing lasts, I guess. It can't, not with animals like that Injun Jimmy Jumper running around loose to lay waste to another man's woman and leave her lying out in the open for the chickens and hogs to do terrible things to her the same as he did to her."

56

Cimarron watched in silence as Jordan again pulled his handkerchief from his pocket and furiously wiped his eyes.

"Eunice saw him to it, Deputy. Go on up to the cabin. It's over that way. Talk to Eunice. She'll tell you what he did."

"I'll do that, Jordan. But first let me say I'm truly sorry about what happened to your wife."

"They'll get him. The vigilantes will. I'd like to be there to see it when they do. I hope they fix it so that Jimmy Jumper dies hard like some broken-necked old dog."

"I can understand how you feel, Jordan, but I got to tell you that the vigilantes' way of handling things like this is the wrong way, and I intend to put them out of business just as fast as I can. I intend to see to it that the law—"

"Don't you try talking law to me, Deputy. Not unless it's lynch law you want to talk."

Cimarron abruptly turned and made his way back across the field. He freed his horse, boarded it, and headed in the direction in which Jordan had pointed earlier.

When he reached the small log cabin, he got out of the saddle and, leaving his bay with its reins trailing, went up to the door, which hung on leather hinges that were badly rotted. He knocked on it, noticing as he did so that the logs of the cabin were badly in need of chinking. The butcher paper that had been coated with grease and placed in the window spaces on either side of the door was torn in several places.

"Who is it?" a feminine voice called out from behind the cabin door.

"Name's Cimarron. I'm a deputy marshal." A moment later, the door opened a crack and Cimarron saw a blue eye in a thin slice of a pale face staring out at him. "Are you Eunice Jordan?" he asked.

The blue eye blinked. "I'm Eunice."

"Your pa sent me up here to talk to you, Eunice. I met him down in the field."

The door opened wider and Cimarron suppressed the urge to whistle admiringly as he stared at the nubile young woman facing him. She was lithe and slender and almost as tall as he was. Her round face was a blend of childlike innocence and worldly womanhood. Her blue eyes were bright and her nose was as pert as her lips, which seemed to be fixed in a perpetual pout that Cimarron found decidedly provocative. Her wavy brown hair spilled below her shoulders and the sun shining on it set it to shimmering. Her breasts were small and firm and Cimarron suspected she was wearing nothing under her blouse because he could see the impressions her nipples made against the cloth. Her hips were full below her narrow waist and the long skirt of her brown cotton dress did not hide her bare feet or trim ankles.

"Might I come in, Eunice? I want you to tell me what happened the night your mother was ra—murdered."

"I don't want to talk about it. I already talked about it to most everybody around here. I don't like to talk about it."

"Eunice, I'm a deputy marshal and I'm trying to find out who killed your mother."

"You said you were talking to Pa before?"

"Yes, I was."

"And he sent you up here to talk to me?"

"He said you could tell me exactly what happened the day your mother died."

Eunice shifted position and peered over Cimarron's shoulder. He turned and followed her gaze. In the distance, Clay Jordan stood beneath a tree smoking a cigarette and watching them.

"Well, if I got to, I guess I got to." Eunice turned and disappeared inside the cabin.

Cimarron followed her inside and found her sitting on a wooden stool near the fireplace. He sat down on a chair near her. "Tell me what happened, Eunice."

"It was Jimmy Jumper who did it. He came here to court me. He'd been coming on and off for nearly a year. Pa was up in Coonsville. Ma and Jimmy and me had supper and then Jimmy and I, we walked out. It was getting dark. He started pawing at me like always, only I wouldn't. He got mad and said he didn't see why we had to wait until we got married and I told him we did and that was all there was to it. We got into a fight and I thought he was going to rip my clothes clear off me. I fought him and then I ran away into the barn and

58

hid. He called me but I wouldn't answer. Pretty soon he went away.

"Well, I waited a spell and then I came out of the barn and started back here to the cabin. When I got here, the door was open and there was a lamp lit inside. I could see them—their shadows—on the butcher paper in that window right there. It looked like they were fighting. Then I heard Ma scream. Then she came running out of the cabin with Jimmy right behind her. I was so scared that I just ran back into the barn. I watched Jimmy catch Ma and throw her down on her back on the ground. He climbed on top of her. He hiked up her skirts until they were up around her hips and then he—he got down on her and started a-humping away.

"It was over pretty fast. Ma got up and she yelled at him. She said she was going to tell Pa what he done to her and then wouldn't there be hell to pay. Jimmy just looked at her. Then he turned around and went into the cabin, and when he came back out, he had Pa's hog-butchering knife in his hands. Ma tried to run, but he caught her easy. He stabbed her more times than I could count. Sometimes I can still hear her screaming." Eunice's hands rose and covered her ears.

After a minute, she continued. "I should have tried to help her, but I was so scared. I hid in the barn and I didn't come out until late the next day when I saw Pa come driving up in our wagon. I ran out of the barn and told him what I'd seen happen. That's all."

Cimarron watched Eunice twirl her hair around her right index finger as she stared into the ashes of the fireplace. She told her story, he thought, like she had it memorized . . . or as if she'd told it lots of time before, as she said she had done. She looked like she wanted to cry and didn't know how to.

"Eunice, are you sure it was Jimmy you saw that night? Could it have been anybody else? Maybe Jimmy went home after you and him had your little spat, and somebody else came into the cabin and—"

"It was Jimmy. I got good eyes. Pa says I'm like a cat because I see good in the dark. Are you after Jimmy?"

"I am."

"So are the vigilantes. They'll kill him. They killed a deputy who came to Wewoka and who was supposed to protect Jimmy. Are you going to kill Jimmy?"

"Not unless I have to."

"Killing him won't bring my ma back."

"That's true enough, but when a man does what you say Jimmy did, the law's got to punish him." Cimarron hesitated a moment, thinking, and then added, "Was your ma a strong woman, would you say, Eunice?"

Eunice got to her feet and went to a wooden cabinet that stood on one side of the fireplace. She opened it, rummaged about in it for a moment, and then turned to Cimarron. She held out a photograph to him.

He took it and looked at the decidedly attractive woman in the photograph; she was tall and well-proportioned. Her hair was piled in a profusion of curls on top of her head and held in place with a tortoiseshell comb. Her large eyes stared up at Cimarron and the slight smile that parted her sensuous lips seemed to mock him. She was standing beside a buckboard, one hand resting lightly on it, the other holding the gathered folds of her long black skirt. To her high-necked white blouse was fastened a small cameo.

"Your ma?" Cimarron asked, glancing at Eunice.

"Yes. She was strong, I guess. She hauled water and fetched wood. She weeded the fields right alongside Pa. Why?"

"I wonder how come she couldn't have fought Jimmy off when he came after her. I mean like you did."

"I don't know. How am I supposed to know a thing like that? She hit him a couple of times. I saw her do that."

"But he got the best of her."

"I told you how it was."

"I'm surprised, since he was courting you, that he didn't try harder to—to take advantage of you instead of going after your ma."

"You can be surprised all you want to be, Deputy. It don't

make no never-mind to me. My ma's dead. Jimmy's gone. I just wish I could go somewheres. To Kansas maybe."

"Why can't you?"

"Pa wouldn't hear of it. I'm only seventeen."

"Lots of women marry by the time they're seventeen."

"Pa's got powerful notions about what's right and what's proper, and a seventeen-year-old girl going to Kansas all by her lonesome, as far as Pa's concerned, is neither right nor proper. So I have to stay put."

"You have a hankering to see some of the world, do you?"

"I just want to get away. From what happened. From what might happen."

"What do you reckon might happen?"

"Somebody—you or Pa or the vigilantes or all of you thrown in together—is going to kill Jimmy."

"I told you I won't. Not if I can help it, I won't."

Eunice met his gaze and Cimarron thought he saw a spark of life flare in her lovely blue eyes, but if he had, it had abruptly died and now she was staring at him in that dull way that seemed characteristic of her and that tarnished the beauty of her face.

"You still love Jimmy."

"Ye—" Eunice flushed crimson and looked down at the floor. She shook her head vigorously. "How could I love a man who did what he did to my own ma!"

"I reckon you've got a point there."

"Anybody home?" called a male voice from outside the cabin. "I give you greeting, Clay. Eunice, are you two inside there?"

"That's Reverend Forbes," Eunice said. "He comes to try to comfort us now and then since . . . you know."

A short middle-aged man as round as a full moon appeared in the doorway. He was wearing a black broadcloth suit, a white clerical collar, and a round-crowned, flat-brimmed black hat. His pudgy fingers were clasped over his bulging paunch. On his rosy face was a broad smile and his black eyes twinkled from between the thick folds of flesh surrounding them.

"Ah, Eunice, my dear. How nice to see you again. But you have company. I didn't mean to disturb you."

As Reverend Forbes started to retreat, Eunice rose and said, "This here's not company, Reverend. It's just a deputy marshal come to talk to me about Ma's murder."

"Sir," said Reverend Forbes, offering his hand.

"Name's Cimarron."

"A truly terrible thing," Forbes said dolefully as Cimarron shook the reverend's soft hand. "A shocking occurrence. Are you here to see justice done, Deputy?"

"I am."

Forbes sighed soulfully. "Jimmy Jumper was a member of my church in Wewoka. It saddens me to see how far the poor boy has fallen." Forbes reached into his pocket and pulled out several folded pieces of paper. "Tracts, Eunice," he explained, offering them to her. "I hope they will help to soothe your soul."

Eunice took them and tossed them on the table.

"Promise me you'll read them, Eunice," Forbes pleaded. "They contain words from the Good Book. They tell how Our Lord taught that we must turn the other cheek to our enemies and how we must forgive—"

"Would you turn your other cheek, Reverend, and forgive a man who did to your ma what was done to mine?" Eunice asked, her voice low, almost a feral snarl. Without waiting for an answer, she continued, "Well, I won't! Not if I live to be a hundred. *Two* hundred!"

Forbes went over to Eunice and began to whisper words to her as he gently patted her shoulder.

Cimarron stood watching, wondering how Eunice could still love Jimmy Jumper—she had almost let it slip out that she did love him still—and yet swear that she would never forgive him for what he had done. Love and hate living in the same nest, he thought. Jimmy Jumper, he thought, had best steer clear of Eunice Jordan.

"Please tell your father I was here," Forbes was saying to

Eunice. "I won't interrupt him at his work. Show him the tracts I brought for both of you to read. And, Eunice, my dear, try not to harbor hate in your heart. It is a worm that gnaws until only pain and corruption can live there, not the love the Lord wants us to have for one another."

Eunice turned her back on Forbes.

He gave her a hurt look and then left the cabin.

Cimarron followed him outside, and as Forbes climbed into his surrey, he freed his bay and swung into the saddle.

"Are you returning to town, Cimarron?"

"I am."

"Do you mind if I ride along with you?"

"Not at all."

As the two men traveled east along the southern bank of Wewoka Creek, Forbes sadly clucked his tongue.

"Something wrong, Reverend?" Cimarron inquired.

"I'm afraid I'm rather a failure," Forbes answered sorrowfully. "In my ministry I try to preach love and brotherhood, and yet we have been plagued by acts of violence committed by the vigilantes in this area. I was so sorry to hear of the death of that other deputy, particularly so because it occurred in what I consider to be an almost sacrilegious manner. And now the vigilantes are intent on finding and, I fear, killing poor Jimmy Jumper."

"Would you happen to know where I might find Jumper, Reverend? I've been asked by his daddy to see to it that the boy don't go and get himself killed by the vigilantes the way Cassidy did."

"I'm sorry, Cimarron. I don't know where Jimmy is. I wish I did. I would very much like to talk to the boy. He needs Christian counseling at this time of crisis in his young life, though I'm not sure he'd listen to me. Not too many of my people do these days, as I said before. You heard how Eunice spoke to me. You heard the contempt she felt for me and for what I had to say to her. People today—all too many of them, I have discovered to my sorrow—do not want to hear the word of the Lord preached in their presence. It is these troublesome modern times, I suspect, that are leading people down the dark path of temptation, and I, in the face of this disturbing fact, am an ineffectual old fool, I fear.''

Cimarron gave Forbes a sidelong glance.

''They think I don't know what life is like—how difficult it can be at times to avoid the pitfalls of sin. Sometimes I find myself wishing that I could tell them the stark truth about myself. That I am not, for example, always successful in driving lust from my own heart and mind. That I sometimes long to indulge in the pleasures of the flesh. That I hold grudges. That I do not always love my neighbor.

''But, were I to tell them that, they would have even less faith in me as a messenger of the Lord than they do now. If they knew that I sometimes want to kick up my heels at a barn-raising and dance until dawn, that I would like to imbibe wine until my head reels . . .

''You'll keep my secrets, Cimarron?''

''Sure, I will, Reverend.''

''If people knew how often I have wrestled with Satan and lost to him, they would despise me, I am certain.''

''Maybe they wouldn't. Maybe they'd come to see that you're a man much like any other who's got his foibles and who's not above occasional folly.''

Forbes seemed not to have heard what Cimarron said. He continued, ''I am a man whose faith sometimes wavers, Cimarron. I freely confess my failing. Do you know the *Rubaiyat*?'' Forbes, in a solemn voice, quoted, '' 'Myself when young did eagerly frequent Doctor and Saint, and heard great argument about it and about: but evermore came out by the same door wherein I went.' So it is with me, my friend. Questions plague me. The answers elude me. I have only my shaky faith, which seems, at times, to stand on only sand.''

''You know the part about the poorly made bowl?'' Cimarron asked.

''I believe so, yes. I love the *Rubaiyat*. My mother named me after its author. My given name—it's Omar.''

Cimarron quoted, ''After a momentary silence spake some vessel of a more ungainly make; 'They sneer at me for leaning all awry: What! did the hand then of the potter shake?' ''

Forbes gave Cimarron a shy smile. "I think I see your point."

"Most people lean awry now and then, I've noticed. I know I do. But don't the Good Book say that the Lord don't care any the less for sinners who slip off the straight and narrow path?"

"He loves most the lambs that have strayed and then returned to the safety of the fold."

"I reckon that's what I was trying to get at."

Later, as the two men rode into Wewoka, Cimarron's attention was caught by a gathering of people clustered around a man standing on a crate in front of the mercantile. As he came closer to the man, he recognized him as the photographer, Elmer Bennett.

He drew rein as Forbes halted his surrey and both men listened as Bennett continued to harangue the small crowd of men and women standing in the street.

"Every man and every woman," Bennett was saying, "has a right to privacy and an equal right to live their lives in the way they see fit without any interference from self-appointed moralists who call themselves vigilantes and wear masks so no one can identify them."

"But no one has the right to live a corrupt life that hurts other people," a woman called out.

"That's Miss Vivian Pruitt," Forbes told Cimarron, "our schoolmistress."

Cimarron, studying Vivian, decided she could be pretty if she'd unpin her hair and let it hang loose and try smiling instead of pursing those lips of hers like she'd just been sucking a lemon. And if she'd loosen her stays, which were hugging her hips into extinction and squashing her breasts like they were overripe melons.

"We have courts, judges, and juries," Bennett shot back at Vivian. "We don't need vigilantes."

"We need decency," Vivian retorted angrily, "and truth and chastity and strict self-discipline in our lives."

"Good day, Reverend," said two Seminole women simultaneously as they came to stand between Forbes's surrey and Cimarron's horse. They had spoken to Forbes but their four eyes were on Cimarron.

"Marshal, we have come to ask a favor of you," announced one of the women who, like the woman beside her, was attractive in a dark, almost mysterious, way.

"A professional favor, Marshal," added the other woman in a throaty voice not unlike that of the woman who had spoken first.

Both women were of medium height and both were buxom and big-hipped, Cimarron noted. Both had smooth dark skin and bright almond eyes. Both had pretty bowed lips, and when they smiled, as they were doing now, their dazzling white teeth gleamed.

"I'm not a marshal," Cimarron told them. "Just a deputy marshal."

"May I present Hannah"—Forbes nodded to the woman who was slightly taller than her companion—"Lewis and her sister, Harriet. The ladies own and operate the mercantile and live in the rear of their establishment. Ladies, this man's name is Cimarron."

"We know," Hannah and Harriet said in unison.

"We heard you were in town, deputy," Hannah said.

"And as we've said, we've come to consult you in your professional capacity," Harriet declared. "A friend of ours just pointed you out to us."

"Ladies," Cimarron greeted them, touching the brim of his stetson to them and giving each of them, in turn, a slow sultry smile.

"I'm very pleased to make your acquaintance, Cimarron," Harriet said.

"I'm absolutely delighted to do so," Hannah said.

Cimarron gave them a grin. "Likewise, I'm sure, ladies."

"The vigilantes," cried Vivian Pruitt from the midst of the crowd, "are trying to instill the same values in the people of this town as I try to instill in their children in school: honesty, integrity, purity."

"But what do you do to your pupils," Bennett shot back, "if they are dishonest or impure?"

"I punish them," Vivian declared pompously.

"How, Miss Pruitt?" Bennett inquired.

"I make them stand in the corner. I give them extra homework. I—"

"But you don't injure or kill them, do you?" There was a smug smile on Bennett's face.

Vivian, flushing, looked first one way, then the other. "Of course, I don't. It wouldn't be—"

"Right, Miss Pruitt?" Bennett prodded.

Vivian fled.

"How do *you* feel about the vigilantes, Cimarron?" Hannah asked.

"My sister and I," volunteered Harriet, "are terrified of them. We've come to ask you to protect us from them."

"We Seminoles," said Hannah, "especially we Seminole women, feel very vulnerable to these marauders. There is, as Reverend Forbes can tell you, a good deal of racial prejudice against us on the part of some whites."

"I'd find it a pleasure protecting two such lovely young women as yourselves, Miss Harriet, Miss Hannah," Cimarron said, and gave each of them a provocative look.

Harriet tittered behind a hand.

Hannah placed a hand on her hip and patted her hair.

Then Harriet said, "We don't want protection just for ourselves, you understand."

"Although we shall both feel quite secure with you looking out for us, Cimarron," Hannah added.

And then they began to speak almost as one. Harriet began, "We Seminoles are having our annual spring festival tomorrow night."

"At Gardner's Grove just north of town on Coon Creek," Hannah continued.

Harriet added, "It might become a rather rowdy affair if past years are any precedent."

"But ever so much fun!" Hannah finished with a saucy wink.

Harriet stepped closer to Cimarron's bay. She crooked a finger at him and he bent down toward her. She looked to the right and then to the left before whispering, "There are rumors that the vigilantes might try to cause trouble at the festival. They do not take kindly to some of our Seminole customs and traditions."

"I heard that, Harriet," Forbes interjected. "I thought the tribal council had decreed against drinking at the festival and also against the 'sacrifices to Venus' that you people have practiced at the spring festival in the past."

Hannah blushed. So did Harriet.

Then Hannah, giving Cimarron a sidelong glance, said, "Reverend, you know very well that my sister and I live exemplary lives all year long—except during the festivals in the spring and autumn. Only then do we surrender to the baser impulses common to all poor creatures made of the base clay into which Our Lord breathed life."

"It is an accepted Seminole custom," Harriet declared. "One of an almost religious nature. Surely the Lord will forgive us our semiannual trespasses when, as Hannah has so correctly pointed out, we live faultless lives the rest of each and every year."

Reverend Forbes harrumphed.

The Lewis sisters looked pleadingly up at Cimarron, who, wondering what the two women had been talking about, said, "Well, ladies, I like a party as much as the next man. But I can't promise you anything. I might not be able to attend, much as I'd like to."

Hannah reached up and placed a delicate hand on top of Cimarron's, which were folded around his saddle horn. "Do try to attend the festival," she said softly. "We'll all feel ever so much more secure if you're there. We need a man like you to protect us and I'm sure you can do that very thing."

"It's no wonder that some of our Seminole men have, since they've seen you about town, taken to calling you Tustenuggee Thlocko," said Harriet. "The name certainly fits you."

"What's it mean?" Cimarron inquired, his curiosity aroused.

"Big Warrior," both women stated in what seemed to be a single voice.

And then, their glances darting up and down his body and giggling, they hurried away and were lost from sight in the crowd.

" 'Sacrifices to Venus' indeed!" spluttered Forbes indignantly.

"What's that mean, Reverend?"

"It is, I fear, merely a fancy name for rutting. As the ladies explained, it is an old Seminole custom practiced at festivals like the one they mentioned. Men and women pair off together and go off into the night and the bushes—"

Cimarron, suddenly understanding what Harriet and Hannah had meant by surrendering to baser impulses and semiannual trespasses, immediately made up his mind to attend the Seminole festival if that proved to be at all possible. It was, after all, he solemnly told himself, his professional duty to help keep order there as he had just been asked to do.

He and Forbes parted, and Cimarron was on his way to Buster Schuyler's livery stable when a young Seminole man stepped down from the boardwalk and seized the bridle of his bay.

"You're Cimarron," the man said tonelessly, looking up at him.

"I am. Who the hell are you? And while you're telling me, get your hand off my bridle."

"I'm called Coacoochee. In your tongue, that means Wild Cat. Jimmy Jumper sent me to find you. He wants to talk to you."

"Where is he?"

Wild Cat gave Cimarron directions to a place east of town. "You'll go and talk to Jimmy?"

"I'll go."

When Wild Cat released his hold on the bay's bridle, Cimarron heeled his horse and galloped east through the town.

5

When he saw the tall tree standing gaunt and alone on the top of a low hill, Cimarron rode up the hill toward it. He passed the tree and then rode down the other side of the hill, following the directions Wild Cat had given him. At the bottom, he veered to the left and entered a grove of pin oaks.

"Hold it right there, Deputy."

Cimarron drew rein and sat his saddle, not turning toward the sound of the man's voice that had come from behind him. "That you, Jumper?"

"It's me."

As Jimmy Jumper, on foot, walked past Cimarron's bay to take up a position some distance in front of the horse, Cimarron studied the man. Young hothead, he thought, noting Jumper's flashing black eyes and the way his hands were twitching at the end of his long lean arms. Wiry. Strong. Thin lips. Arched eyebrows just as thin. He's itching for action, he thought. Look at the way he all but dances in place where he's standing there looking up at me so cocksure of himself.

"I heard," Jumper said in a steady tone, "that you were fixing to wet-nurse me like that other deputy tried to do."

"Your daddy thinks you might get yourself in trouble if somebody doesn't look out for you, Jumper. From what I've been hearing, your daddy's right."

"I didn't kill Mrs. Jordan and I sent for you to tell you that."

"Eunice Jordan told me she saw you rape and murder her mother."

"Eunice is lying. I don't know why she's lying, but she damn sure is lying."

"Now, why would she lie about a thing like that? I got the idea you and Eunice were real close."

"We were close. I don't know why she lied. I wasn't even in town the night Mrs. Jordan was murdered, let alone anywhere near the Jordan place. I was up north of Coonsville on business."

"What kind of business?"

"Tribal business. I went to see a rancher up that way, a man who sells beef to the Seminoles."

"What's his name?"

"Sloan. You can go talk to him. He'll tell you I was there, all right."

"Why didn't you say so—tell somebody?"

"Never got the chance. The vigilantes came after my ass before I could tell anybody, except Cassidy. He was going to check out my story, but the vigilantes killed him before he got a chance to."

"Let's go, Jumper."

"I'm going nowhere with you, Deputy. I just sent for you to tell you I was innocent and to tell you you'd be wasting your time hunting me down for crimes I never did commit."

"Innocent or guilty's not the main point right now, Jumper. Keeping you out of the unfriendly hands of the vigilantes— that's the main point. I'm taking you back to Wewoka with me and I'm going to find someplace safe to store you until I can get my hands on the men who murdered Cassidy."

"I can look after myself, Deputy," Jumper assured Cimarron. A scornful smile spread across his square face. "I don't need wet-nursing. It's about time us Seminoles started looking out for ourselves. It's also about time we started doling out some of the same medicine to those white-bellied vigilantes who've been giving us Indians so much trouble."

71

"Jumper, don't talk foolhardy. You've got yourself a good job, your daddy told me, with the tribal council. You're young and you've got your whole life, or most of it anyways, to live yet. Powerful people—at least one I know of—speak highly of you."

"Who?"

"August Child, according to your daddy."

"That bastard!" Jumper spat.

"Your daddy said that Child is a member of the tribal council and that he gave you your job as tribal bookkeeper. You want to turn important men like that against you, do you?"

"August Child's not fit to lick my spit."

Jumper's vehemence surprised Cimarron. "What's got you so down on a man I was told is your benefactor?"

"You want to know why I was up in Coonsville to talk to that rancher, Sloan?"

Cimarron waited.

"Because I was checking the tribal books one day and I couldn't make them balance. I went over and over them—annuities received, payments made—the whole month's figures. Well, finally I figured out why the books wouldn't balance. August Child had turned in bills that were supposed to be from Sloan for beef he sold to the council, only they didn't fit with the records of beef received and distributed.

"What it all boiled down to in the end, I found out, was that August Child was taking money from the tribal till and turning in false statements of account from suppliers like Sloan to cover up what he was taking. I went back over the books for the whole year and found the selfsame thing. Don't you talk to me about him being my 'benefactor' and such like. August Child's nothing but a thief and a son of a bitch who's selling his own people down the river."

Cimarron nodded. "That may well be so, Jumper. But it don't in any way alter the fact that I told your daddy I'd look out for you so you don't get yourself killed. Now, enough of this talk. Let's move out."

Jumper said, "Make me move out. You think you can?"

Cimarron sighed and got out of the saddle. He strode up to the unarmed Jumper. "I'm through arguing with you, old son." He swung a hard right that slammed into Jumper's jaw.

As Jumper staggered backward, he whistled shrilly through his teeth.

Three Seminoles materialized out of the shadows lurking in the grove. Three revolvers pointed at Cimarron.

Jumper, massaging his jaw, said, "I told you, Deputy, that it was time us Seminoles got a little starch in our spines, not to mention some guns in our hands. Did you know that last night the vigilantes burned the cabin of one of our women out on Tiger Creek because they said she was whoring?" Without waiting for Cimarron to respond, Jumper continued, "Our Lighthorsemen aren't worth a tinker's damn; they're never there when you need them. Besides, the Seminole police have no authority over white men who commit crimes here in the Nation!"

"How do you know for sure that the vigilantes are white?" Cimarron asked.

"You think they're Seminoles? *Seminole* vigilantes? Deputy, you've got more imagination than brains." Jumper laughed mirthlessly. "Go back to town, lawman. We don't need your help. We'll take care of ourselves and our people—us Red Sticks will. There are five of us so far, including me and Coacoochee."

Jumper pointed to the man nearest him. "Ya-ha-hadjo—Mad Wolf." He singled out a second man. "Ye-how-lo-gee—Cloud." Pointing to the third man, he said, "Fuch-a-lusti-hadjo—Black Dirt." Then, turning back to Cimarron, he said, "Red Sticks, all of them."

"Red Sticks? I don't follow you, Jumper."

"The Red Sticks were a warrior society in the old days. It's pretty much died out since the Removal, but the Red Sticks were a force to be reckoned with back in Florida, as your white brothers, should you ever ask them, will tell you. Now, we know that the vigilantes want me. Well, to get me, they'll have to reckon with me and my fellow Red Sticks here. If there's blood to be spilled, I can tell you true it won't all be Seminole blood. Some of it'll be out of the veins of whites. If you're bent on catching yourself some vigilantes, Deputy, you'd best be about it real quick because us Red Sticks, we've got the selfsame notion. Now, you ride on out of here so we don't have to start our shooting match with you as our first target."

Cimarron, standing stiffly, flicked his eyes from Jumper to the three silent men who were still aiming their guns at him. Jumper's unarmed, he thought. Maybe I could make a grab for him, use him as a shield . . .

As if divining Cimarron's thoughts, Jumper stepped backward out of his reach.

Cimarron turned, got back into the saddle, and rode out of the grove of trees. Abruptly, he drew rein, turned in the saddle, and shouted Jumper's name, intending to try one last time to reason with the man.

A bullet whined through the trees, snapping off a slender branch.

He heeled the bay hard and rode away, cursing Jumper and the other Seminole Red Sticks who were so hell-bent on setting out on the warpath against the vigilantes.

After leaving his bay in Buster Schuyler's livery stable, Cimarron made his way through the thickening shadows of late evening to the Wewoka Social Club.

Inside it, he sat down at a table near the counter that served as a bar and beckoned to the man behind it.

"What can I do for you, Deputy?" the man asked uneasily as he arrived at Cimarron's table.

Elmer Bennett, seated at a nearby table, answered the bar dog's question by saying, "You can tell him to get the hell out of thish town if he knows what'sh good for him."

Cimarron gave Bennett a cursory glance and then ordered whiskey. As the bar dog went to get it, Bennett got unsteadily to his feet, nearly knocking over his chair as he did so, and, picking up his bottle and glass, weaved over to where Cimarron sat watching him approach.

"*Ummphh,*" Bennett muttered as he sat down heavily

across from Cimarron and banged his bottle and glass down on the table.

"You doing some celebrating?" Cimarron inquired, noting the photographer's bleary eyes and slack mouth.

"Nope. Drowning my sorrows."

"They dead yet?"

Bennett grinned lopsidedly. "Most of 'em. Business is bad. I mean, how many weddings or christenings can take place in a hamlet the size of Wewoka? How many new babies are born for me to photograph so that their doting parents can preserve the image of their mewling offspring for a posterity that probably won't give a damn in a few more years?"

The bar dog appeared and placed a bottle and glass in front of Cimarron. "Elmer, why don't you go home and sleep it off?"

"The night'sh young yet," Bennett declared, and filled his glass.

"And you're as drunk as a deacon already," observed the bar dog. "Deputy, if he's bothering you . . ."

Cimarron shook his head and the bar dog returned to his station behind the counter.

"Cimarron," Bennett said, "you getting much lately?"

"Getting much of what lately?" Cimarron asked as he filled his glass and drank from it.

"You know." Bennett giggled. "You getting to fire that gun you got dangling between your legs?" When Cimarron didn't reply, Bennett continued, "I happen to have something that might console you in your lonelier moments, Deputy."

Cimarron put down his glass and met Bennett's eyes, waiting.

Bennett thrust a hand into his inner coat pocket and withdrew an envelope, which he dropped on the table. "Open it," he told Cimarron. "Go ahead."

Cimarron did. He stared at the first photograph on the top of the pile that had been in the envelope.

It pictured a thin woman who was completely naked and standing facing the camera, her legs spread at an awkward angle, both of her hands lifting her sagging breasts so that their nipples seemed to be peeking shyly at the camera. On her drawn face was what Cimarron supposed was meant to be an inviting look but it looked to him like a parody of a licentious leer.

"Pretty good, huh?" Bennett emptied his glass.

Cimarron flipped through the other photographs. All of them were of the same naked woman in obscene poses. In some, she was alone. In others, she was with one or, in several cases, two men.

"Look at that one," Bennett directed, reaching out and extracting a picture from the pile Cimarron had replaced on the tabletop. "Now, that one's enough to make any man who's not past ninety or dead pop right up, raring to have a go at the nearest thing that will let him plug it, be it woman, man, or beast of the field."

Cimarron stared at the picture Bennett was holding only inches from his eyes. In it, the woman was on her knees, bending down over a man lying supine on the wooden floor. Her mouth enclosed him so thoroughly that her lips were pressed tightly against his thick thatch of pubic hair. Another man, also on his knees and behind the woman, was taking her anally, his large hands clasping her hips to pull her close to him.

"Shots like these are a sideline of mine," Bennett announced, and then hiccuped. "A man hash to make a living the besht way he can." Bennett discarded the photograph and chose another. "How about thish one, Deputy? What does thish one do to you?"

Cimarron stared silently at the photograph Bennett held up for his inspection. In this one, the woman was lying on her back on the floor. Kneeling directly above her head was one of the two men who had been in the other photograph. The woman's right hand gripped his erection as her lips totally enveloped his testicles.

"Just the thing to have with you when the nights are long and your bed is empty," Bennett said, smirking. "They're for sale. Five dollars apiece."

"I'm not buying, Bennett."

"You don't like my artistic handiwork? Those pictures don't start you tingling down where it counts most?"

"I like to do, not look."

"Well, sure, you do, Deputy. I can tell that just by looking at you. You're obviously a man of action. But there are timesh when a man can't do. Timesh when, for one reason or another, he can only look. That's where these come in." Bennett tapped the pile of pictures with a fingernail. "*Four dollars apiece.*"

"The lady—she a friend of yours?"

"She was a whore who worked the Wewoka Hotel for a while before moving on." Bennett emptied his glass and, leaning close to Cimarron, whispered conspiratorially. "I've got quite a collection of pictures like these in my studio. And not all the women in them are whores like her." Bennett's fingernail impaled the wan woman in the photographs on the table. "If I ever decided to make my collection public—let me tell you, it would be the day the roof blew off thish town." Bennett chuckled drunkenly. "Whew!" he exclaimed, rising unsteadily. "Time for me to hit the hay before it hits me." Without another word, he staggered out of the social club.

The bar dog came up to Cimarron, shaking his head. "Elmer's going to get himself into trouble one of these fine days with those pictures he's been peddling, you mark my words."

He picked up Bennett's bottle and glass, but before he could leave the table, Cimarron asked, "What might you mean by that remark?"

"Elmer was in here the other night, with his pictures. He was showing some of them to another man. Andrews was his name, Ken Andrews. Andrews had drifted into town a few days earlier looking for work, and he finally found it. He's been working as a field hand for August Child, whose farm is due west of where that deputy was crucified.

"Well, sir, Bennett sold Andrews some of his dirty pictures and Andrews kept taking them out of his pocket and looking at them and putting them back and taking them out again once Bennett had gone home drunk. He showed them to Clay Jordan, who came in here later that night, and Clay—that man can be as righteous as a teetotaling preacher—didn't want any part of them.

"Clay treated them like they were a piece of shit he'd picked up by mistake, and I remember he told Andrews that Bennett, in his lofty opinion, ought to be struck dead by the good God for what Clay called 'his abominations.' Now, that's what I mean by Bennett had best watch his step. I'm not saying that Clay Jordan's a vigilante, but I am saying that the vigilantes, whoever the hell they are, don't take kindly to what they consider sinning. Why, only yesterday—last night, to be exact about it—they burned the cabin of a young Seminole woman out on Tiger Creek because there's been talk in town lately that she'd taken to entertaining men for money."

"Heard about that," Cimarron said, thinking of Jimmy Jumper and his Red Sticks. He paid the bar dog for the whiskey he had drunk and then left the social club.

Once outside, he made his way along the boardwalk in the darkness that had descended upon the town. He had almost reached the hotel when he heard a low moan that came from an alley on his left. He halted, listened.

The moan came again, louder this time, and Cimarron peered into the shadows choking the alley. With his hand on the butt of his .44, he eased into the alley, his eyes wide open to sharpen his night vision. He almost fell over the body on the ground before he saw it.

He hunkered down beside the man and turned him over.

"Lost," murmured the man. "My way. Help—"

"Bennett? That you?"

"My studio—where—"

Cimarron hauled Bennett to his feet, threw the man's right arm over his shoulders, and holding him by the wrist, walked him out of the alley and into the light of the gas lamp burning on the corner. "What happened to you, Bennett?"

"Drunk as a skunk," Bennett muttered, and giggled giddily. "My studio—"

Cimarron walked Bennett, who was an almost total dead-weight as a result of his drunkenness, toward it. When they reached the photographic studio, Cimarron asked, "You got a key?"

"Pocket."

Cimarron let Bennett slide down into a sitting position against the outer wall of the studio and then he searched through the man's pockets until he found the key. He unlocked the door and, after hauling Bennett into a reasonably upright position once more, marched the man inside.

Cimarron guided Bennett into the rear room, where he found, by the light of the moon shining through the room's single window, a bed. He released his hold on Bennett and the photographer crumpled in a heap on the bed.

As Bennett, suddenly sound asleep, began to snore, Cimarron dropped the key on a table near the window and made his way back into the studio at the front of the building. He was reaching for the door when it suddenly flew open to admit a number of shadowy figures who came rushing into the room, nearly knocking Cimarron to the floor as they did so.

The door slammed.

"Grab him," somebody snarled. "He's here. I just bumped into the bastard!"

"Got him!" somebody yelled, and Cimarron struggled in the darkness to free himself from the man who was pinioning his arms behind his back.

"Help me hold him," the man struggling with Cimarron yelped.

Cimarron suddenly backed up several swift steps, slamming the man who was holding him against the wall and causing him to let out a roar and release his hold. As another dim figure sprang toward him, Cimarron threw a left and felt it glance off the man's burly shoulder. As the man he had swung on tried again to grab him, the deputy seized the figure he realized was wearing a loose robe and a hood over his head and spun him around before sending him careening across the room to crash into a table, splintering it.

Cimarron reached for his gun, but before he could unleather it, someone jumped on his back and someone else, coming up on him from his left flank, raised something Cimarron couldn't quite see and brought it crashing down.

Cimarron's head screamed with the pain of the blow. He reached out with his right hand and seized his attacker's weapon, which, he realized, was a leg of the broken table. Swinging it in a wide arc, he backed toward the door, holding the robed and hooded vigilantes at bay.

They all stood motionless for a moment, shadows crouching within shadows, and then they began to move slowly toward him while remaining just out of reach of the table leg he was wielding.

Cimarron shifted his weapon to his left hand and reached for his Colt.

But before he could draw his gun, the door was suddenly thrown open and it slammed hard against his back, sending him staggering across the floor and into the arms of several of the vigilantes, one of whom tore the table leg from his hand.

"Heard the ruckus you boys were making," said the vigilante who had thrown open the door. "Figured you might be having some trouble with him."

"Take him into the back room."

The vigilantes dragged Cimarron into the back room. Someone lit a lamp.

Someone else cried, "That's not Bennett!"

"It's that damned deputy," a gruff voice declared.

"There's Bennett!"

One of the vigilantes went to the bed and pulled the still-snoring Bennett to his feet.

"What—who—" Bennett cried, his arms flailing helplessly.

Cimarron, held by two of the vigilantes, tried to break free and received a stiff fist in his midsection by a third man, a blow that ripped the breath from his lungs and left him bent over and gasping.

"Jesus Chirst!" the suddenly sober Bennett cried as his eyes finally focused and darted from one hooded figure to the next. "You boys, what do you want here?"

"You, Bennett," said the gruff-voiced vigilante.

"Me? What have I done? I haven't done anything—nothing that would warrant you boys coming after me. I swear it!"

"Where are they?" the same vigilante asked Bennett. "The filthy pictures—where are they?"

"What filthy pictures?"

"Where do you keep them?"

Bennett's frantic eyes swerved to a wooden cabinet that stood beneath the sink. One of the vigilantes silently pointed at it and another one bent down and opened it. The man extracted a folder from the cabinet, opened it, and shook its contents out onto the table.

Cimarron stared down at the obscene photographs that littered the table. The men and women in them, as the flickering flame of the lamp played upon them, seemed to be alive and moving as they engaged in their lewd acts.

"Destroy them!" shouted one of the vigilantes.

Obeying the order, one of the men removed the globe from the lamp and held the photographs, one after the other, in the flame until nothing remained of them but a small pile of charred ash on the tabletop.

"We're here tonight, Bennett," said one of the vigilantes, "to make sure you don't take pictures of that ilk ever again." The man gestured, and the two men holding Bennett forced him down into a chair.

As pain from the blow he had received on his temple cannonaded through his skull, Cimarron said, "You got a complaint about Bennett, gents, you ought to take it to the law."

The vigilantes ignored him.

"What are you going to do to me?" Bennett asked, his voice little more than a whimpering whine.

The two men standing behind his chair, who were gripping his arms, shifted position slightly. Bennett cried out from the pain of their tightened hold on his arms.

One of the vigilantes stepped forward to stand directly in front of Bennett. "We're going to fix you so you won't take any more filthy pictures, that's what we're going to do to you. Then we're going after Ken Andrews, who bought some

81

of your abominations from you.'' The vigilante's right hand shot toward Bennett's face.

Bennett swiftly swung his head to the side.

"Hold him steady,'' barked the man standing in front of Bennett. "His head—hold it steady!''

A third vigilante appeared behind Bennett and gripped Bennett's ears with both hands, immobilizing the photographer's head so that he was forced to stare straight ahead of him.

"Listen to me," Bennett cried, his eyes wild and his face a pale mask of terror. "I'll leave town. You'll never see me again!''

The vigilante confronting Bennett ignored the outburst and once again his hand shot toward Bennett's face. This time, his aim was accurate, since Bennett could not move his head.

Cimarron's stomach lurched within him as he watched the vigilante's fingers claw at Bennett's left eye as if seeking purchase on its slippery surface. Cimarron struggled in vain to free himself from his captors, unable to look away from the vigilante's first two fingers as they gouged Bennett's right eye out of its socket.

His ears were assaulted by Bennett's agonized shrieking. As the vigilante hurled Bennett's bloody eyeball to the wooden floor, Cimarron swallowed hard and his stomach continued to heave. He found himself transfixed by the sight of Bennett's uprooted eye, which lay, bloody and with pale strings of muscle attached to it, on the floor. The eye seemed to watch the ghastly proceedings with an unnatural calm, the calm of dead flesh no longer under the control of a human brain.

Bennett's screams, louder now and more awful, caused Cimarron to look up in time to see the vigilante's bloody right hand tear Bennett's left eye from its socket and hurl it from him as if it were something sickening.

Bennett's eye hit the wall and bounced off it, to land on the tabletop. There, it rolled, leaving a trail of blood behind it, before reaching the edge and plopping down upon the floor below.

"Let him loose," ordered the vigilante, stepping back

from Bennett and wiping the gore covering his hands on his black robe.

The three men who had been holding Bennett withdrew, and Bennett, shrilly screaming still, shot to his feet, his hands flying up to his face and the empty sockets streaming with blood where his eyes had once been.

Bennett staggered first one way, then the other. As he collided with one of the vigilantes, the man shoved him away, causing Bennett to fall against another of the vigilantes, who also pushed him away. It became a game. Bennett, the ball; the vigilantes, the ball players.

They pushed him. They kicked him. They sent him screaming and twirling, a demented dervish, from one pair of hands to the next and then on to the next.

"You'll take no more filthy pictures," bellowed the vigilante who had blinded Bennett. "And by the time we're through with Ken Andrews, he won't be able to get any kick out of looking at your disgusting pictures."

"What are we going to do with this deputy?" one of the men holding Cimarron shouted in order to be heard above the ear-shattering sound of Bennett's screams.

"We'll take him with us," the gruff-voiced vigilante replied. "Let's go now before the whole damned town shows up here to find out why this blind bastard is making such a racket."

The men holding Cimarron shoved him toward the back door and then through it. "Where are we going?" one of them asked.

One of the vigilantes pointed into the night. "Follow me," he muttered.

Cimarron was half-carried, half-dragged through the night and away from the sound of Bennett's screams, which had become a kind of bubbling torrent of sound that rose, fell, rose, and abruptly fell again.

Cimarron tried to trip one of the men dragging him through the darkness. He tried to kick the shin of the other man who was holding on to him.

Suddenly, the vigilantes stopped; Cimarron looked around him but could see nothing except the distant backs of the buildings that lined the main street of Wewoka. Lights were burning in some of them. Others remained dark.

Bennett could still be heard wailing in the distance. Beneath his tormented lament could be heard the sound of his body as it banged blindly into walls, furniture—a thudding, crashing sound punctuated by screams that were interspersed with his wild wailing.

"The cistern," said the gruff-voiced vigilante.

"We're going to drown him?" one of the others asked with muted glee in his voice.

"We don't want him wandering around loose, now do we? Not after tonight, we don't."

"But he don't know us. He can't identify any of us."

"He's out to get us—don't lose sight of that fact. On account of that other deputy—that Cassidy. Throw him down the cistern."

As the two men shoved Cimarron forward toward the circular stone wall of the cistern, which he was now able to see dimly in the distance, he fought them but failed to free himself. They reached the cistern, and Cimarron thrust out both booted feet and braced them against its wall.

The two men holding him suddenly pulled him away, and then, as if by some unspoken but prearranged signal, they bent the top of his head down and hurled him forward.

As his head struck the cistern's stone wall, his hat fell off and the pain the blow caused was added to the pain that still lurked within his skull as a result of the earlier blow he had received.

His captors pulled him backward. They slammed his head against the cistern's wall a second, shattering time.

Cimarron's skull exploded in a shower of lights that burst red and white within it before they, like Cimarron himself, went hurtling down into the cistern toward its dark water far below.

6

As Cimarron struck and then plummeted below the surface of the cold water in the cistern, consciousness returned to him with the force of an explosion. His mind responded to the danger of drowning by galvanizing his muscles into a struggle upward through the water in search of lifesaving air.

As he broke the surface of the water and gasped desperately in an effort to draw air into his lungs, his fingers clawed at the slimy stone sides of the cistern's circular wall. He found no purchase anywhere and felt himself, because he was weighted down by his waterlogged boots, being drawn down into the depths of the water again. Frantically, he clawed at the stones that formed the wall, his fingernails breaking as he again slipped far below the surface of the water.

He fought the urge to open his mouth, knowing that only water, not air, would enter it. He struggled against the strongly instinctive but, he knew, decidedly deadly impulse to breathe.

His shoulder struck the wall as he tried to fight his way up to the surface, and his legs thrashed wildly, slamming with slow force because of the weight of the water—against the side of the cistern, causing pain to sear his left kneecap.

His fingers again scraped at the rough stones of the cistern's wall, but he could not get a grip on their smooth and slippery surface.

Panic nearly engulfed him as his lungs, about to burst for

lack of air, burned beneath his ribs. With a supreme effort of will, he brought his knees up and, at the same time, reached behind him until his palms touched the wall. Bracing his boots against the wall in front of him with his knees bent at a sharp angle, he pressed his back against the wall behind him and then, with the help of his hands, began to ascend toward the surface of the water.

His progress seemed to him to be no progress at all. Instinct suddenly dominated him. His mouth opened. Water flooded into it. At the same time, he began to take in more water through his nose.

His body slipped downward, but his brain screamed a command that forced him to continue his torturous ascent.

Suddenly his head was above water and he was coughing and spitting desperately. Water flew from between his lips. He gasped, tears streaming from his eyes as a result of the fire that was consuming his lungs. His chest inflated. He coughed again. More water sprayed from his mouth. He sucked in air through his wide-open mouth and flaring nostrils as he remained almost immobile, except for his labored breathing, his back, hands, and boots pressed against the wet stone wall of the dark cistern.

He didn't know how much time had passed before, finally, his breathing approached a nearly normal rhythm. He tilted his head back and looked up the tall tunnel that was the cistern. He saw a starry sky that seemed to be a world away, a sky that was circumscribed by the cylindrical mouth of the cistern.

He pressed his hands against the wall as hard as he could and then eased his back up the wall. He withdrew one booted foot and positioned it higher on the wall. Then he raised his other foot and planted it as firmly as he could beside the first.

He repeated the maneuver a second time. And then a third.

He looked up. The stars seemed no closer to him. He swore and tried again.

His left hand slipped on something slimy growing on the stones. His right foot, seized suddenly by a cramp, fell away from the wall.

He let out a demonic yell, a sound full of fury and frustration, as he fell with a splash down into the water. He was again beneath its surface and he was again trying to fight his way back to the dry world of life-giving air for which his lungs were shrieking.

When his head broke the surface of the water less than a minute later, his frantically clawing hands dislodged a large stone from the wall; it plopped into the water below. He thrust all of his ten fingers into the empty space where the stone had been and hung suspended, half in and half out of the water. He let his head rest on his upper arms as seconds and then minutes passed and his breathing gradually returned to normal. Then, he let go, threw himself backward, and at the same time thrust his legs forward until he had again attained the position he had been in before with his back, hands, and boots pressed against the wall.

Concentrating hard on every cautious move he made so that he would not slip again, he began to ease up the wall toward the stars so far above him.

Hands, he thought, and moved them upward. Feet, he thought, and moved them gingerly, one at a time, slamming one boot and then the other against the stones as if they were battering rams. Back, he thought. And slid his body upward, feeling first his shirt and then his skin tear as he did so.

He settled into a steady silent rhythm, concentrating on each small move he made toward his destination. Hands, feet, back, hands . . .

The stars above him, as he raised his head to stare up at them, seemed to be slowly descending toward him.

Hands, feet, back, hands, feet, back . . .

Barely daring to breathe, he continued his upward journey and almost cried out in exultation when he felt and then saw the insteps of his boots come to rest on the rim of the cistern's wall. He gave one final shove with his hands and then he straightened his body and held it rigid. He spanned the mouth of the cistern; his boots jutted over the edge and his bleeding back rested upon it. He drew a breath and then rolled to the right. He fell, his body hitting the ground hard, and then he lay still, his right cheek pressed against the grass, which was wet with dew. Gratefully, he breathed the night air through his nose and mouth, smelling its sweetness, tasting its freshness.

Some time later, he raised himself to his knees. He shook his head and water flew from his hair. His shirt hung down in wet bloody shreds, touching the grass on both sides of his trembling body. He sat down and pulled off his boots. He poured water out of them before pulling them back on. Then he got shakily to his feet and stood with his buttocks braced against the stone wall of the cistern, staring into the night at the buildings in the distance.

He heard no screams and wondered what had happened to Bennett.

He saw no lights in the buildings and wondered whether, if he had shouted for help, anyone would have come or if they all would have remained within their homes, afraid to come to his aid because the night was infected with roaming vigilantes.

He bent down and picked up his hat, almost losing his balance as he did so. Clapping it on his head, he began to walk toward the buildings in the distance, a name resounding in his mind.

Ken Andrews.

The vigilantes, he recalled, had told Bennett that they intended to get Andrews for having bought some of Bennett's photographs. Groggily, he remembered that the bar dog in the social club had said that Andrews was working for August Child as a field hand. The man had also mentioned that Child's house was due west of the spot where Cassidy had been crucified.

Cimarron, intending to track down and warn Andrews of the vigilantes, made his way to Bennett's photographic studio. He entered it by way of the still-open back door, apprehensive about what he might find inside. He found nothing. There was no sign of Bennett. The lamp still burned on the table and there was blood everywhere—on the furniture, the floor, the walls. He called Bennett's name. No answer. He searched the building. Empty.

He left the studio by the front door and made his way to Schuyler's livery stable. He pounded with both fists on its closed door until it was opened by a sleepy-eyed boy.

"Need my horse," he told the boy as he brushed past him and entered the livery.

"You're hurt," the boy said as he stared at Cimarron's bloody back. "Mister, you look like you're hurt real bad. What happened to you?"

"Had the misfortune to run into some of your town's upstanding citizens who run around in the dark wearing robes and hoods."

"Vigilantes?"

Cimarron nodded. He went to his saddlebags, which were draped over the wall of the stall, and opened one. His bay stood inside the stall as sleepy as the boy behind him.

"They tried to kill you, mister, the vigilantes did?"

"They tried, but they didn't try hard enough." Cimarron took a clean shirt from his saddlebag and then stripped the ruined one from his body. After removing his badge from the shredded shirt and pocketing it, he used the rag to wipe the wetness—a combination of water and blood—from his back before putting on the clean shirt.

"Why did the vigilantes come after you, mister?"

"Because they know I'm out to get them. And I will get them even if hell turns out to be standing between me and them."

Cimarron discarded his useless shirt. He got the bay ready to ride and then went galloping out of the livery and up the main street of Wewoka.

As Cimarron, on his way to August Child's house, came out of the grove of trees into the clearing where Cassidy had been crucified, he suddenly drew rein. He sat his saddle, staring at the naked body that had replaced Cassidy's on the two crossed planks that still sprouted from the ground like some grotesque and lifeless tree.

Moonlight spilled down upon it. Silence shrouded it.

As the body moved slightly and moaned, Cimarron dug his heels into the bay's ribs. When he reached the man, he slid out of the saddle and went up to him, his eyes dropping to the gaping rent in the man's flesh that was at the apex of the V formed by his spread legs. His eyes dropped even lower, and he stared at the man's severed genitals, which lay on the ground, moon-slicked, bloody, and covered with buzzing flies and silent black ants.

Cimarron pulled his bowie knife from his boot and then tried to ignore the man's moans of pain as he pried out the nails that impaled the man's hands and feet on the planks. As gently as possible, he laid the man down on his back on the ground.

He had never seen him before, but he was almost positive he knew who he was.

"No more—oh, please, no more!"

"I'm not going to hurt you. I'm here to help you. Are you Ken Andrews?"

The man nodded weakly. "The vigilantes . . ."

"I know." Camarron reached out and retrieved Andrews' shirt from the pile of clothes that lay near the severed organs. He gently placed the crumpled cloth between Andrews' legs and then silently swore as the blood that was still spurting from Andrew's wound began to turn the shirt into a red morass.

". . . because of the pictures Elmer Bennett sold me."

"I know," Cimarron repeated.

"She was beautiful." Andrews eyes slid slowly shut. "In my pocket—pictures. See for yourself."

"Not now, Andrews. I've got to get you to town—to a doctor." How'm I going to do that? Cimarron wondered. How in the hell am I going to do that without Andrews here bleeding to death on me before I've gone so much as a mile?

"Get pictures—my pants pocket."

When Cimarron made no move, Andrews tried to prop himself up on one elbow, but he was unable to do so.

"I'm ugly as sin," he said, his voice a soft sigh. "Some've

said I was plain. They were being kind. No woman wanted me . . ." His voice faded and then grew suddenly strong. "But I wanted them—even ones as ugly as me. Oh, I hurt so *bad*!" Andrews' left hand rose, wavered above his body a moment, and then came to rest on the shirt Cimarron had stuffed between his legs.

"I liked to look—the mail-order catalogs—the women in their corsets and things." Andrews laughed, a chocked mirthless sound. "It ain't right what they done to me, mister. I couldn't get a woman of my own. So I looked. The pictures were all I had. Now I'm dying on account of them. I know it. You know it. Let me look—please, mister—one last time."

Cimarron pulled Andrews' pants toward him and searched through his pockets until he found the photographs. He removed them from Andrews' pocket and held one of them up in front of the mutilated man at an angle so that the moonlight illuminated it.

Andrews sighed, his eyes wide. "Ain't she something?" His eyes shifted to Cimarron and then seemed to go out of focus. "Look, mister. Ain't she the prettiest thing you ever laid eyes on?"

Reluctantly, Cimarron looked at the picture of the nude woman he was holding up. His body stiffened as he recognized the woman, who stood in a coy pose that concealed nothing, a smirk on her attractive face.

"Elmer didn't tell me her name," Andrews said softly. "Said she paid him to take these pictures of her. He said she wanted them to give as a gift to her lover. Elmer said he made some extras to sell and I was sure glad he did."

"Andrews, did Bennett tell you who this woman's lover was?"

"No." Both of Andrews' hands clutched his savaged groin. He groaned and quickly withdrew his hands from the now thoroughly blood-soaked shirt Cimarron had placed on his wound.

"Andrews, the bar dog in the social club told me he saw you show these pictures to a man in the social club in town."

"They made him mad—he called me names, stormed out of the place."

"Did you know the man you showed the pictures to?"

"No." Andrews' eyes glazed.

"Did you show these pictures to anybody else?"

When Andrews, his eyes closed, didn't answer, Cimarron leaned down toward him and repeated his question.

"No," Andrews answered. He grimaced. "My hands—my feet—those nails—"

"I'm going to get you up on my horse," Cimarron told him. "It's going to hurt you bad, but I've got to get you to a doctor." He pocketed the pictures and slid his hands under Andrews' body.

Andrews made no sound, no move. He's fainted, Cimarron thought. He lifted Andrews, and as he did so, the bloody shirt fell to the ground. Cimarron looked down and then he lowered Andrews to the ground. He hasn't fainted, he realized. He's died. He stared down at Andrews' groin and saw that the blood no longer spurted out of his body: the man's heart had stopped pumping it.

Cimarron climbed into the saddle and rode due west. When he reached August Child's house, he dismounted in front of an imposing two-story brick structure with verandas on both the first and second floors. He went up to the front door and knocked soundly on it several times before lamplight began to stream from an open second-story window.

The lamp and a woman's white-nightcapped head appeared in the window. "Who is it? Who's down there?"

"I'm looking for August Child. He to home?"

"I'm Mrs. Child. Mr. Child isn't here. What is it you want? I'm sure I can't help you. I can't answer your questions. Go away and come back when my husband is here."

"I've got some bad news to tell your husband, Mrs. Child."

"I told you I can't help you. You'll have to talk to my husband."

"There's no need for you to be so flighty, Mrs. Child. I'm not here to cause you any trouble. I just want to . . ."

Cimarron left his sentence unfinished as he heard the sound of a horse's hooves in the distance, shattering the otherwise still night.

"That might be— Yes, it is. It's Mr. Child. Talk to him. Maybe he can help you with whatever it is you want. I can't." Mrs. Child and her lamp disappeared from the window.

Cimarron stepped down from the veranda as August Child rode up to the front of the house and dismounted.

Child was a fat-faced and benign-eyed Seminole whose thick shock of black hair persisted in falling down across his forehead despite his almost constant efforts to brush it back into place.

"I don't believe I know you, sir," he remarked, his eyes on Cimarron. "May I ask what you are doing here at my house at this hour?"

"I'm here about Ken Andrews. Heard he worked for you."

"Yes, he works for me. He lives in a small cabin behind the house."

"He don't work for you anymore, Child, and he don't live in your cabin anymore. He's dead. The vigilantes got their hands on him." Cimarron explained what had happened to Andrews and Child's response was a wordless exclamation that signaled both shock and dismay.

"I take it you weren't home tonight, Child."

"No, I wasn't. I had some business in town to take care of, and it took far longer than I thought it would to conclude it satisfactorily."

"Andrews, I reckon, must have done some screaming while those vigilantes were working him over. Maybe your wife heard something."

"I'll ask her." Child disappeared inside the house, and when he reappeared a few minutes later, he was shaking his head. "She heard nothing."

"Did Andrews have any wages due him?"

"Yes, he did. Why?"

"Then maybe you'll use what's due him to pay for his burying."

"Yes, I will. Of course, I will. But I'd have seen to the matter even if I owed the poor man no money at all."

Cimarron noted the distress on Child's face and he found himself wondering if this man, who seemed so stricken at the news of Andrews' death, could really have stolen annuity money from his tribe as Jimmy Jumper had so angrily alleged. But that's none of my affair, he told himself. If Child's a thief, the fact remains that it's a case of an Indian committing a crime against other Indians, which leaves me out of the picture. It's up to the Seminoles to settle the matter among themselves according to their tribal law. He thought of Jumper again and wondered if the man would observe the niceties of tribal justice. He doubted it.

"Deputy," Child said as Cimarron was about to step into the saddle, "there has been so much trouble in this area lately because of the vigilantes. I wonder—we—the Seminoles are having our annual spring festival tomorrow night. A few of our Lighthorsemen—those that are here in Wewoka—will be in attendance in an attempt to keep order if that should prove necessary. But our police have no authority where whites are concerned. If the vigilantes were to cause trouble at the festival . . . You see, it is not an entirely, shall we say, innocent affair. It has distinct overtones of sexuality related to the fertility rites practiced by our people many years ago, the vestiges of which still survive among many of us, especially at such a time as the spring festival and the one celebrating the harvest each autumn."

"I take it you're asking me to help your Lighthorsemen oversee the affair."

"You are a deputy marshal with duly constituted authority here in Seminole Nation," Child commented pointedly.

"Two ladies I met—sisters—they already invited me to come to the shindig you folks are having tomorrow night."

"Hannah and Harriet Lewis?"

"They're the ones." Cimarron looked up at the sky, which was paling with the light of false dawn. "The festival you folks are having *tonight*, I should say. I'll do my best, Child, to oblige you, but I'm not promising you I'll be there. I've got me some vigilantes to catch for assorted crimes they've

94

committed, and I've also got to get my hands on whoever it was killed Clementine Jordan."

"Jimmy Jumper killed her. Eunice Jordan was a witness to the crime."

"So I've heard. Well, I'll be heading back to town now, Child."

"Let me thank you sincerely for coming here to tell me about Andrews. I'll retrieve his body and see to the obsequies this very morning."

When Cimarron awoke, his hotel room was dark, and for a moment he was not sure where he was or what time it was. But then, remembering, he got out of bed and lit the lamp on the table by the window.

He poured water from a pitcher on the bureau into a porcelain bowl and washed his face, hands, and upper torso.

He stood staring at himself in the mirror for a moment, thoughtfully running his right hand down along the stubble covering his cheeks and chin. Then, retrieving his bowie knife from his boot, he soaped his beard and used the knife to scrape away the stiff, dark stubble.

He dressed and left his room. In the lobby, he glanced at the clock above the registration desk, which read eleven minutes after nine.

He left the hotel and made his way to the livery stable. As he entered it, Buster Schuyler, who was busily filling feed bins with oats and hay, looked up at him in surprise, spilling oats on the floor as he did so.

"You," Schuyler breathed.

"Me," Cimarron said, and pointed to the spilling grain.

Schuyler hurriedly righted the sack in his hands. "The word around town is that the vigilantes had killed you last night."

"The word's wrong, though they did try to kill me." Cimarron entered the stall that housed his bay, and taking his saddle blanket from the stall wall, he shook it out and then draped it over the bay's back.

He was saddling the animal when Schuyler said, "You're a lot luckier than that other deputy was."

"Luck had little to do with it," Cimarron said bluntly as he bridled the bay. He turned toward Schuyler. "You sound disappointed that the word you heard around town's not true."

"No, no, it's not that. It's just that I'm surprised you survived, that's all."

"Schuyler, since you seem to hear about everything that's going on here in Wewoka, maybe you can tell me something."

"I will if I can."

"Did Clementine Jordan have a lover?"

"A lover? Mrs. Jordan? Not likely."

"You mean you would have heard about him if she did."

"No, I mean Clay Jordan wouldn't let any man come within a country mile of his wife, he was that jealous of her."

Cimarron led his bay out of the livery.

Schuyler followed him. "Did she have a lover—Clay's wife?"

Cimarron swung into the saddle and looked down at Schuyler, whose eager expression betrayed his prurient interest. "I'm on my way over to Jordan's place now to ask him the very same question."

"You never can tell about people, can you?" Schuyler asked rhetorically as Cimarron walked the bay away from him.

When Cimarron reached the Jordan place, he dismounted and, noting the lamplight streaming through the window, went up to the door and knocked on it.

Eunice Jordan gave a little cry when she opened the door a moment later.

"What's wrong?" he asked her.

"You. Pa said the vigilantes had killed you last night."

"They didn't. Your pa shouldn't pay attention to wild rumors. They can addle a man's mind. Is he to home, Eunice?"

She shook her head. "He's out."

"Out where?"

Eunice shook her head again. "I don't know where Pa goes or what he does."

Cimarron hesitated a moment and then, drawing a deep breath, asked, "Would you say your ma was a clean-living woman, Eunice?" He thought he saw an expression of what might have been distaste—for his question?—flicker across Eunice's face, but it was gone, if it had ever really been there, in an instant.

"Isn't it enough that she's dead?" Do you have to go around running her good name down into the mud?"

"Be seeing you, Eunice," Cimarron said. He touched the brim of his hat to her, not bothering to point out to her that she had not answered his question.

He climbed aboard the bay and headed for Coon Creek, thinking of Hannah and Harriet Lewis and hoping.

He heard the sounds of the festival shortly after he had forded Tiger Creek and started north along the bank of of Coon Creek. There was laughter, male and female, and someone singing tunelessly. A fiddle shrilled.

As he rode into Gardner's Grove, which was ringed with parked wagons, surreys, and picketed horses, he was suddenly cut off by two mounted Seminoles, both of whom were carrying revolvers.

He drew rein and said, "I'm a deputy marshal and I've been invited to this party by August Child and the Lewis sisters."

"Cimarron!"

He turned to see Roley Jumper hurrying toward him through a band of revelers near the bank of the creek. He raised a hand in greeting.

"He's all right," Jumper told the two Seminoles as he came up to Cimarron. "He's one of Judge Parker's deputy marshals."

The two Seminoles, still silent, turned their horses and rode away.

"Lighthorsemen?" Cimarron asked.

Jumper nodded. "Have you found Jimmy?"

"I found him. He wanted no part of me. Him or one of his Red Stick friends sent a bullet my way."

"Then my son remains unprotected," Jumper exclaimed. "The vigilantes—"

"You son's got himself a notion that he can protect himself with the help of his Red Sticks."

"But we Seminoles no longer have an active Red Sticks warrior society."

"You're wrong there, Jumper. Your boy's gone and resurrected it. So far, he's got three men on his side—at least three that I saw—and him and they've got themselves a notion to tangle with the vigilantes, which may or may not turn out to be such a good idea."

"Isn't there anything you can do to help Jimmy?" Jumper pleaded, anguish evident in his eyes.

"There might be. I might be able to get my hands on Jimmy and hide him out somewhere until I've had a chance to put the vigilantes out of commission."

"You will still try to help Jimmy, then?"

"I will."

Jumper turned at the sound of his name being called by a man on the far side of the fire. "Excuse me, Cimarron. And let me assure you that you have not only the thanks of a grateful father, but also his apology for the bullet you said was fired at you either by my son or by one of his companions."

When Jumper had gone, Cimarron dismounted and, after tethering his bay to a nearby tree, walked over to the fire that was burning on the bank of Coon Creek. He searched the firelit faces but Hannah and Harriet Lewis were nowhere in sight. One familiar face smiled up at him. The man waved.

He walked up to where Possum Jack Tucker sat cross-legged near the fire, a portly Seminole woman seated beside him.

" 'Evening, Mister Deputy," Possum Jack greeted him, the beads of sweat on his black face shining in the light of the fire. "You be welcome to sit with me and my missus if you've a mind to."

98

"I thank you kindly." Cimarron hunkered down beside the black man and his wife.

Possum Jack spoke in the Seminole language to his wife, who got quickly to her feet and scurried around the fire. She was back moments later. In her hands were a plate heaped high with food and a cup, both of which she handed to Cimarron.

"Dig in, Mister Deputy," Possum Jack said. "They's no trace of possum to be found here tonight, but that there venison is passable." He laughed. "I do dote on possum meat. Catches possums, I do. Been treeing them ever since I was knee-high to a gnat. That be why folks call me Possum Jack."

Cimarron picked up a chunk of roasted venison and ate it. "Good," he said, nodding at Possum Jack's wife, who was beaming at him. "Great," he said a moment later as he gnawed on a roasted rib. "I'm kind of surprised to see you here, Possum Jack. I mean, since you're not a Seminole and this here's a Seminole festival. I was invited. You were, too?"

"I *am* a Seminole, Mister Deputy," Possum Jack declared proudly. "When the war end, I be adopted by the tribe along with all the rest of us black folks that used to be Seminole slaves."

Cimarron began to devour a hot corn cake smeared with jelly. "Real sweet stuff," he said pointing to the jelly.

"We call it conte," said Possum Jack's wife, still beaming at Cimarron. "It is good, yes?"

"Sure is," Cimarron agreed, licking a stray streak of jelly from one of his fingers.

"It good to be a free man," Possum Jack mused dreamily. "Old Roley Jumper or his daddy don't own me or mine, not no more they don't. But they owned my daddy and his daddy before him, not to mention me. The old days, they was hard. I can surely testify to that. Roley Jumper could be a mean man and so could his daddy, once they got a whip in one hand and a nigger in the other. Drink up, Mister Deputy."

Cimarron picked up the cup he had placed on the ground in

front of him and drank some of its contents. His lips twisted and he grimaced.

Possum Jack's wife giggled. "That is cazina," she told Cimarron, tapping his tin cup with a fingernail. "We make it from a bitter weed as we once did in the east. It is good."

Cimarron put the cup down.

"The missus and me," Possum Jack said, "have our own place now and we're filling it up with maroons. Four so far."

"Maroons?" Cimarron glanced at the black man.

"That's what the Seminoles call mixed-bloods. Seminole/white. Seminole/black. Like that. White folks' word be 'mulattoes.' Call 'em what you will, those chilluns of ours is a blessing, and they will be more so of a one as me and the missus gets to be on in years. And they's *free*! They's even official members of the Seminole tribe like me. I tell you, Mister Deputy, I am one glad man that I be living in these good days and be near to forgetting I was ever old Roley Jumper's—and his daddy's before him—slave."

"Cimarron, there you are!"

Cimarron looked over his shoulder to find Harriet Lewis hurrying toward him, her sister at her side.

"How wonderful to see you again, Cimarron," Hannah cried as he got to his feet. And then both women were talking at once, something about dancing.

He handed his empty plate to Possum Jack's wife. "Much obliged, ma'am. That was real tasty."

"Enjoy yourself at the festival," she told him.

"People, they do," Possum Jack said, a sly smile on his face. He pointed and Cimarron saw a man leading a woman into a dark part of the grove.

"I saw him first," Harriet hissed at her sister as a Seminole fiddler began to play and couples began to dance. "Come along, Cimarron," she said, firmly taking his arm. As she hurried him over to where the dancers were grouped in front of the fiddler, he looked back over his shoulder at the pouting Hannah and gave her a wink, noting as he did so that Possum Jack and his wife had disappeared.

And then Harriet was in his arms and they were twirling

100

and twisting, his boots thudding on the hard ground, her skirts swishing around his legs.

Was she? He wasn't sure, but Harriet seemed to be pressing her body against his. It's the dancing that makes her do it, he thought. Or is it? He held her more firmly and much closer to him.

She smiled up into his eyes.

The fiddler fell silent.

Hannah appeared and announced, "My turn." Pushing her sister aside and shouting, "Play!" to the fiddler, she put her arms around Cimarron. As the fiddler obeyed her imperious command, Cimarron held her close as they danced, happily conscious of her firm breasts pressed against his body and blissfully aware of the way her pelvis pounded against his own.

"Let me lead," she whispered, and before he could object, she was leading him around the fire. And then, to his delight, she clasped his hand and went running toward the trees.

He ran behind her, listening to the grunts and sibilant sighs that seemed to be coming from everywhere in the dark grove, the sounds of lovemaking by invisible lovers hidden from the moon and the stars by the sheltering branches of the trees.

Hannah suddenly halted, released Cimarron, clasped his head between her hands, and kissed him passionately. When her lips withdrew from his, she said, "I wanted to do that the first time I saw you. So did Harriet; she told me so. The instant we saw you, we both decided that you would be the one with whom we would commit our semiannual transgressions. Harriet and I simply live for our spring and autumn festivals. In town, people watch and tongues wag. But here, now, it's altogether different. No one raises an eyebrow at *anything* anyone chooses to do." She kissed him again and continued kissing him as his hands came to rest on her breasts.

Around them in the darkness drifted fireflies and the sighs and moans of men and women making their lusty Seminole sacrifices to Venus.

"Come . . . this way," Hannah whispered huskily. She

led him to a secluded spot and began to unbutton her blouse.

Moments later, her breasts were free and a moment after that Cimarron was sucking the right one as Hannah's hot hand massaged him and he sprang into quick stiff life.

He paid no attention to the sound of someone crashing through the underbrush nearby as he switched to Hannah's left breast and she unbuttoned his jeans and slid her hand in to capture his throbbing erection. She released him after giving him one final squeeze. Pulling up her skirt and lowering her undergarments, she lay down on the ground on her back and held up her arms to him.

Cimarron dropped to his knees, hurriedly unbuckling his cartridge belt, which he placed with his hat beside Hannah. He slid his jeans down and was about to drop down on Hannah when two hands seized his shoulders from behind.

"Hussy!" a voice hissed in the darkness.

Cimarron recognized Harriet's voice.

"You broke the rules," she snapped at her sister. "We agreed that the one who saw him first would be the first to—"

But Harriet stopped abruptly and leaned over to whisper in Cimarron's ear.

Following her eager orders, he obediently pulled off his boots and then his jeans. He slipped his shirt off, dropped it, and lay down on his back on the ground.

Harriet knelt between his legs. Her head lowered and her lips parted. He sighed softly as he watched his erection disappear into her hot mouth, and he sighed again and then groaned with pleasure as her head began to bob up and down upon it and his testicles began to tingle.

He looked up as Hannah dropped to her knees and crawled toward him. He smiled at her as she bent her head. Her tongue touched his left nipple, then his right. It slid down along his belly as her fingers toyed with his nipples and her sister continued making wet gurgling sounds as she continued to suck his shaft, her head bobbing up and down, her fingers caressing the insides of his thighs.

102

"My turn!" Hannah said, and pushed her sister aside.

As the two women switched positions—Hannah's mouth embracing him and Harriet's lips laving his bare torso— Cimarron felt himself surging toward a climax. The sisters continued to service him, Hannah's tongue teasing him and Harriet's hand embracing his testicles. And then, as Harriet continued to fondle his testicles and as Hannah's tongue continued to swirl about his stone-stiff erection, someone screamed—a woman.

And then a man was shouting and the sisters quickly withdrew from Cimarron, fright disfiguring their faces.

"What is it?" Hannah asked nervously, and Harriet, as if in answer to her sister's question, screamed, "Vigilantes!"

Cimarron leapt to his feet as the masked, robed, and mounted riders came crashing through the trees. "Run!" he told the sisters. "That way—back the way those bastards came from!"

Their skirts flying out behind them, Harriet and Hannah ran through the grove as more screams erupted from countless throats and people began to run in all directions. The mounted vigilantes, wielding whips, lashed out with them at both men and women.

7

Cimarron made a grab for his clothes, and as he did so, the end of a bullwhip snaked out and circled his wrist.

The vigilante holding the whip's stock jerked it upward and Cimarron was pulled forward several feet and then thrown to the ground.

Tearing at the whip, he managed to free his hand. He got to his feet as the vigilante's horse circled him and the vigilante drew back the bullwhip, ready to strike a second time.

Cimarron turned and ran toward his clothes, his eyes on his holstered Colt, which lay beside them. He never reached them. He was cut off by a second vigilante who was whooping loudly and whirling the whip in his hands above his head as if it were a lariat.

Cimarron skidded to a barefoot halt, but before he could head in another direction, he felt a whip slash his buttocks. He let out an angry roar and turned, but a fleeing Seminole, his hands flying wildly in front of him, collided with Cimarron and knocked him to the ground.

"It's that deputy again," one of the vigilantes shouted above the screams and ululations arising all around Cimarron as the Seminoles fled on foot, in wagons, and on horseback from the site of their festival. Looking at the mayhem, Cimarron saw some of the Seminoles were as naked as he was, others clothed but just as frantic in their desperate attempt to escape. The vigilantes seemed to be everywhere, as if they were as numerous as the silent fireflies that still sparked the night with their little lights.

Cimarron scrambled to his feet to find four vigilantes, two of them armed with whips and two of them with revolvers in their hands, converging upon him from all directions.

Between one of the vigilantes and Cimarron lay his cartridge belt with its holstered revolver and his clothes.

Run!

The word roared in his mind. He ran. Dodging the fleeing Seminoles and the four vigilantes who were after him, he ran, not sure where he was going, knowing only that he had to get away, had to somehow save himself, and knowing too that the two vigilantes with the guns would not hesitate to shoot him.

One of his pursuers fired at him. He heard the bullet whine past him before *thunking* into a nearby tree trunk. He ran on, in a deliberately erratic fashion to avoid being hit by vigilante bullet or whip, his breath coming fast, his heart pounding, his feet hurting as they were torn by the sharp underbrush.

Low-hanging branches whipped his face and brambles tore at his body as he fled north, with Coon Creek on his right a wide wet expanse in which the light of the moon seemed to be drowning, turning the creek's surface silver as it did so.

"Get the bastard!"

Cimarron recognized the gruff voice of the man who had blinded Bennett. He ran on, swerving and dodging trees that suddenly loomed in front of him as if intent on impeding his flight.

He kept to the trees to slow the vigilantes' pursuit of him, but soon they began to thin out and then finally gave way to mere pointed stumps, and he thought, beavers.

Beavers felled these trees to build their dam.

The dam, he thought as he came out into the open. Saw it on my way into Wewoka. Where? *There!*

He raced toward the creek, the sound of the vigilantes crashing through the trees a distant sound behind him.

When his bleeding feet touched the cold creek water, he

dived headlong into it and swam below its surface toward the beaver dam, which was just ahead of him. When he reached it, he dived downward and began to feel along its rough underwater surface, which was composed of mud, branches, and bark.

Fighting the impulse to surface for air, he continued searching until he found the entrance to the beavers' lodge.

Not wide enough, he thought, his lungs about to burst within him.

He tore sticks and branches from around the opening to widen it. Moments later, he was able to squeeze into it. Wriggling upward for what seemed to him an eternity, his head finally broke the surface of the water inside the lodge. As he gasped for breath, scurrying sounds filled the total blackness of the lodge.

He reached up and then, treading water, turned and felt along the wall of the lodge behind him.

An unseen beaver scraped his hand and he quickly jerked it away.

A moment later, he heard the splashes that he knew meant that the beavers were deserting their lodge, abandoning it to him, the rude intruder who had so suddenly invaded their domain.

He finally found the narrow ledge he had been searching for, the one on which the beavers rested, high and dry, from their dam-building labors.

He pulled himself up on it and, as he did so, his shoulders and back scraped the top of the lodge. He gingerly turned over on his back and began to claw at the ceiling of the lodge, tossing the sticks and branches he dislodged into the water, only inches below him.

Soon he had made enough room for himself so that he could lie prone and breathe easily. He lay without moving in his refuge as his breathing slowly returned to normal.

They're out there, he told himself, those masked bastards, beating the bushes and trying to find me. He smiled in the impenetrable blackness that surrounded him. That's the second time they've tried to turn me into dead meat, he thought as the water in the lodge lapped gently against the edge of the beavers' sleeping platform on which he lay. *I've got to down them before they take a notion to try for me a third time.*

He closed his eyes. Time passed. He dozed, but jerked awake at the sound of a splash and the feel of a furry wet and clawed body climbing over his own. He let out a yell and swung an arm, striking the beaver that had entered the lodge and sending it plopping back into the water.

More time passed.

He thought of Harriet and Hannah Lewis and what the sisters had been doing so skillfully to him when the vigilantes had raided the festival. Remembering, he silently damned the raiders for interrupting the ladies and ending the ecstasy he had been experiencing as a result of their eager efforts. One more score to settle with those vigilante sons of bitches, he thought angrily.

Some time later, he roused himself from an erotic reverie involving Hannah and Harriet and decided it was time to leave the lodge. Working slowly but surely, he began to dismantle a portion of the roof, tearing out branches and twigs and keeping his eyes and mouth closed as gobbets of dried mud fell down upon him. As he dropped the beavers' building materials into the water below, they made an almost rhythmic succession of small splashes.

When he was able to thrust his hands through the opening he had made, he hurriedly widened it. The darkness of the night outside was not nearly as dark as the interior of the lodge had been. He sat, then stood up on the beavers' sleeping platform and looked around.

The damned creek lay still in the moonlight. There were no vigilantes in sight. The only sound was the vaguely mournful cry of a nightbird somewhere in the distance.

He climbed up on the roof of the lodge and then, on hands and knees, began to crawl along it toward the bank of the creek. When he reached it, he jumped down upon it and went loping south toward the cover of the trees.

Once under their branches, he slowed his pace and moved

cautiously and nearly soundlessly through the trees, heading back to Gardner's Grove.

He found his cartridge belt where he had left it. It took him several more minutes of searching to find his clothes and hat, which had evidently been kicked by running feet or galloping hooves.

He dressed and went to where he had tethered his bay, passing an overturned wagon with a broken wheel as he did so. His horse nickered as he approached it. He spoke softly to it and then ran his hand gently down the animal's neck. The bay turned its head and nuzzled his shoulder. He freed the animal, swung onto the horse, and headed south, saddle leather creaking beneath him as if in response to the sounds of nocturnal insects. Fireflies swarmed around him. A mosquito landed on his cheek and he slapped it away.

Wewoka was silent as he rode down its gaslit main street some time later. He drew rein when he saw a tall pole; it had not been there before, but now it sprouted in the street directly in front of Buster Schuyler's livery stable. It sported a coat of fresh red paint that gleamed like blood in the light of a nearby gas lamp. Now, what the hell's that supposed to be or mean? he wondered.

No answer came to him. He rode on, halting in front of the mercantile and dismounting. He wrapped his reins around the hitch rail and then went around the side of the building. At its rear door, he knocked softly. When there was no response to his knock, he tried again, more loudly this time. Still no response.

"Harriet," he called out. "Hannah! It's me, Cimarron!"

Silence.

He simultaneously pounded on the back door and called the women's names. He was about to give up and leave when he heard a bolt being shot and then the door opened a crack. "Hannah? Harriet?"

"Go away!"

"Honey," he whispered to the invisible Harriet through the crack in the door when he recognized her voice. "Let me in and let's you and me and Hannah finish what we started out at the grove tonight."

"No," Harriet snapped. "Go away! The vigilantes have warned everybody!"

"Warned everybody about what?"

"*You!*" The second voice he had just heard, Cimarron realized, was Hannah's, but he could see neither her nor her sister. "They've spread the word that they'd make serious trouble for anybody who has anything at all to do with you."

"Go away," Harriet repeated. "And don't come back here—*ever!*"

The door slammed.

Cimarron heard the bolt slide into place. He sighed and walked around the house to the street, aware of the unsatisfied stiffness between his legs. But I can't blame the ladies, he thought. They're scared, and they've got every right to be. He kicked a stone lying in his path and hurt his toe.

"Goddamn you!" he said aloud, staring at the stone but thinking of the vigilantes. Thanks to them, he thought, here I am as horny as a stud horse without a mare anywhere in sight.

And then, suddenly, he remembered the cheerful and willing Mae Holloway. Grinning, he swung into the saddle and headed for her house.

He was surprised to find, as he turned into the side street on which Mae's house was located, that light spilled through the kitchen window. No need to be surprised, he advised himself, though it's well after midnight. Mae's probably entertaining one or more of those gentlemen callers she mentioned to me the day we met. Maybe, if she's in an amiable mood, she'll let me get on line.

When he reached Mae's picket fence, he tethered his horse to it and then crossed the yard and went up on the porch to find that the front door was open. He was about to knock on the screen door when he heard a soft sound that he could not at first identify. But when it came again a moment later, he was sure it was the sound of someone moaning faintly. Someone inside the house. Mae?

"Anybody home?" he called out. "Mae, you in there?"

The moan again.

He opened the screen door and went inside. He stood for a moment in the hall, listening. The hall was filled with light spilling through the open door leading to the kitchen. Cimarron went to the kitchen and his body froze as he stood just inside the door staring at Mae.

She was bound to a wooden chair. She was naked. There was a gag in her mouth held in place by a strip of rawhide wound around her head. Her hair was disheveled. Tears streamed from her eyes as she stared up at Cimarron, and he stared at the burned flesh of her face and breasts where someone had brutally branded her. There was an X on both of her charred cheeks and one in the middle of her forehead. The same mark had been seared into the flesh of both her breasts.

He hurried over to her. "Honey, what the hell happened?" he asked as he removed the rawhide and then the gag from her mouth. "Who did this to you, Mae?" he asked as he quickly untied the hemp rope that bound her hands to the back of the chair.

She tried to speak but couldn't. Her lips moved and she licked them several times until she had gathered enough saliva to wet them.

As Cimarron, on his knees in front of her, untied her ankles, which had been bound to the two front legs of the chair, she said hoarsely, "Vigilantes."

He had known it even before he had asked his question. He rose. "The bedroom. I'll help you to it."

As he helped Mae to her feet, she staggered and almost fell. He picked her up and carried her weeping into the nearest bedroom, where he placed her gently on her back on the bed.

"When did they do that?" he asked, indicating the seared flesh that disfigured her face and breasts.

"I was in bed," she murmured, and turned over on her left side, away from Cimarron. She drew her knees up and covered the exposed side of her face with her right hand. "It was

late, nearly midnight. Someone—at the door. I thought—"
She laughed, a cracked sound. "Do you know what I thought?
I thought maybe it was you, that you'd come back to see me
again. I hoped—I opened the door, they burst in. They tore
off my nightdress, tied me up. They—one of them—had a
running iron. I screamed. They gagged me. They stoked the
fire in the kitchen stove and put the iron in it.

"Cimarron, they said they knew about me and Sean—you
and me, too. They said they'd come to fix me so that no
deputy like you or Sean would want me ever again. You can
see that they did. No deputy, no man will want me, not now,
not the awful way I look. But even so I guess I'm lucky."

"Lucky?" Cimarron asked incredulously.

"They said they were going to blind me. The way they did
Elmer Bennett, but with the running iron this time. I was
terrified. I tried to break free. The chair fell over. They
laughed and picked it and me up again."

"Mae, maybe you are lucky at that."

Mae's body shook as she sobbed, a succession of violent
sounds.

"You're alive, Mae. They didn't blind you. And you're
wrong about nobody ever wanting you after this. Hell, honey,
those brands'll heal up, and once they do, why, they won't be
so noticeable. I'll go get a doctor—you got one in town?"

Mae nodded and told him where the doctor lived. She
turned over on her back. Covering her branded breasts with
both hands, she stared up at Cimarron. "I'll be scarred for
life. Like you."

Cimarron's hand rose and fingered the scar on his face.
"The doc can maybe do something so that your flesh'll heal
without leaving any marks."

"What happened to you?"

"A branding iron left this mark on me. My pa and me, we
were branding calves some years back when I was but a boy.
A calf got away from me and Pa—oh, my, was that man
mad. At me more than the calf. He swung the iron he'd been
heating and it raked my cheek. He didn't mean to hit me with

111

it, it was just that he was so mad and—well, that's what happened."

Cimarron turned and headed for the door.

"That scar," Mae said, and he turned back to face her. "It didn't stop me from wanting you."

"I think I catch your drift, honey. Now, you keep on thinking like that. With a little luck and the help of the doc I'm going to go now and fetch, you'll be fine. Men'll not even notice you're nicked. What they'll notice is those blue—no, gray—eyes of yours and the way they have of making a man want to drown himself in them. They'll notice that pretty blond hair you've got and how it curls. Most of all, they'll notice you're a real fine figure of a woman. And the smartest of them all will notice you're a warm-hearted and friendly type of lady."

"You did?"

"Almost the minute I first met you. For sure, directly after."

"Cimarron, don't go. I'm afraid to stay here alone. They— the vigilantes—might come back."

"They won't," Cimarron assured her, fervently hoping he was right. "They've done their share of dirty work for tonight. Now I'll go get the doc and send him to you. Lock the door once I'm gone, honey."

"You'll come back to see me sometime?"

"Sure I will." He went back to the bed, bent down, and gently kissed both of Mae's savaged cheeks. "I'll come calling on you, if you'll let me, just as regular as a goose goes barefoot."

Mae managed a wan smile.

Cimarron left the house and galloped through the night to summon the doctor, so he could try to repair the damage the vigilantes had done to Mae Holloway because she didn't play life's game by their narrow and restrictive rules.

After he had brought the doctor to her and the man had done what he could for her and gone, Cimarron sat with Mae. He made her a cup of strong tea and a roast-beef sandwich as dawn was breaking, but she accepted only the tea. Realizing that he was hungry, he ate the sandwich himself. Mae finally fell into a fitful sleep. He covered her with a light blanket and then left the house.

He boarded his bay and rode to the hotel, where he left the animal tethered to the hitch rail outside. He was halfway up the steps to the second floor when the sleepy clerk behind the desk awoke and let out a startled cry. Cimarron halted and looked down at the man.

"Sir, please," cried the clerk as he scurried out from behind his desk and came over to the foot of the stairs, "you can't stay here!"

"I can't. Why the hell not?"

"The vigilantes came here last night. They told me that they'd been after you—out at Gardner's Grove—and that you got away from them. They said they knew you were staying here, and they said if you came back they'd make sure this hotel burned to the ground. So please, sir. Try to understand. I'm sorry, but you just can't stay here. I have a wife and two children. If they knew I let you stay here . . . Oh, please, sir, go somewhere else. *Please!*"

Cimarron's shoulders slumped. He reached into a pocket of his jeans, withdrew the iron key to his hotel room, came down the steps, and handed it to the clerk. He paid the man what he owed him.

"Thank you, sir. Thank you very much. I'm sorry, I truly am. But the way things are . . ."

Cimarron strode out of the hotel, the room clerk's words a half-heard buzz in the air behind him. He stood on the boardwalk watching the town come to early-morning life, thinking that any one of the men he saw passing in wagons and on foot might be a vigilante.

His teeth ground together as his gaze shifted among the faces of the men on the street and boardwalk. Because of the vigilantes, he thought, Harriet and Hannah Lewis had come to fear him. Anger raged within him as he realized that he could not return to visit Mae Holloway despite what he had told her. If he were to do so, his visit might incite the wrath of the vigilantes and cause them to inflict further injury upon her. Three women, he thought, and every one of them beyond my reach at the moment on account of the vigilantes. Three more good reasons, he thought, for hunting down those masked men who've rampaged through the lives of so many other people with such awful results, among them Sean Cassidy, Elmer Bennett, and Ken Andrews.

When he noticed the crowd of people that had gathered around the oddly ominous red pole that rose so starkly in front of Schuyler's livery stable, he stepped down off the boardwalk, crossed the street, and joined the crowd.

"Any of you folks happen to know what this thing is and who put it here?" he asked.

He was aware of the apprehensive glances the people in the crowd were giving him. He repeated his question.

"It was some young Seminoles who put it here in the middle of last night," a man in the crowd volunteered. "I was coming home from the social club and I saw them."

"Me, too," declared another man. "They said for us two to tell everybody that they intend to fight back against the vigilantes who raided their people's festival out at Gardner's Grove last night."

"But the pole," Cimarron said, pointing to it, "what's it mean?"

An elderly Seminole man standing on the fringes of the crowd stepped forward. "My people—in the old days in the east they put up poles like that."

When the old man said no more, Cimarron asked, "Why?"

"It was then, and is now, a sign of war. War that the Red Sticks' warrior society will wage against their enemies."

"The vigilantes," Cimarron said, and the Seminole nodded.

"Much obliged for the information." Cimarron turned and recrossed the street. So it's war, he thought as he retrieved and boarded his bay. A war between Jimmy Jumper's Red Sticks and the vigilantes, he thought, with me right in the middle of the fracas that's about to be. He heeled the bay and galloped out of town.

When he reached August Child's house, he dismounted and knocked loudly on the front door.

Child opened it moments later. "Ah, Deputy, it's you again. What can I do for you this time?"

"Child, there's trouble brewing." Cimarron told him about the pole the Red Sticks had erected in Wewoka and about the vigilante raid on the Seminole festival the previous night.

"They raided the festival? Was anyone hurt?"

"Don't know. I came here, Child, to give you some advice, and I hope you'll take it."

"Advice?"

"You're a member of the Seminole tribal council. I figure what you and the other members of the council ought to do is get together and see if you can't find some way to stop Jumper from waging the war he's got it in mind."

"How can we do that?"

"That's not up to me. It's up to you and the other council members. How you do it's no concern of mine, but you'd best do it or there's going to be more blood running in the streets of Wewoka before long. None of it needs to be shed."

"It seems to me that it's your job to stop the impending tragedy, Deputy."

Cimarron noted Child's emphasis on the last word he had spoken. "It's my job, all right, but I can't do it alone. Seems to me you Seminoles in authority ought to get your Lighthorsemen out on the scout to help prevent trouble."

"I'll recommend such a course of action to the council. I'm sure they will be amenable to my suggestion."

"Meantime, I'll do all I can to keep the Red Sticks and the vigilantes away from each other's throats."

Cimarron, after leaving Child's house, searched for a suitable spot to make camp. He passed the spot where the crossed planks still stood and then rode on toward Coon Creek. He had almost reached it when he spotted smoke rising just ahead.

Campfire? He didn't know. He did know that he had a number of enemies in the area.

He drew rein, slid out of the saddle, and led his bay into the trees. He tethered the horse to an oak and then made his way cautiously through the trees toward the spot from which the smoke was rising. He halted as the trees began to thin out, and positioning himself behind one of them, his hand on the butt of his .44, he watched Jimmy Jumper and the other men who were gathered about the low fire.

He counted seven Seminoles in addition to Jumper. Among them were Cloud, Black Dirt, and Mad Wolf, whom he had met during his earlier encounter with Jumper. The boy's got himself some new recruits, looks like, he thought, watching the Red Sticks as they talked earnestly among themselves. His gaze shifted to the three white boys seated on the ground near the fire. Red Sticks? Not likely. Then, who are they and what are they doing, here? he wondered.

And then, as one of new Red Sticks, whose back had been to him, turned, Cimarron saw the revolver in the man's hand . . . the revolver that the new recruit was using to cover the three white boys. The war's started, he thought.

"Don't move, mister!"

Cimarron froze at the sound of the male voice behind him.

"Get your hand off your gun," the man ordered, and Cimarron's hand withdrew from his revolver.

"Raise 'em!"

Cimarron's hands rose.

"Now, let's join the party."

Cimarron moved forward, his hands above his head, and halted when he reached the campfire.

"Well, look who's here!" crowed Jumper, a broad smile on his face. "Where'd you catch him, Wild Cat?"

Wild Cat stepped out from behind Cimarron and said, "Back there in the trees. He was sneaking up on you fellows."

"Well, Deputy," Jumper said, "you're just in time to see some Seminole retribution."

"What're you fixing to do, Jumper?"

"Kill those three whites." He pointed to the three boys seated on the ground under guard. "We rounded them up at sunrise from the farms in the neighborhood."

116

"Why?" Cimarron asked, stalling for time.

"Why?" Jumper's smile faded. "The vigilantes raided our festival last night."

"I know that, but what's that got to do with these three youngsters?" Cimarron was sure that the oldest of the boys was no more than seventeen or eighteen. "You figure them to be vigilantes?"

"Don't know if they are or not," Jumper declared. "It doesn't matter. What matters is that an old Seminole man died of apoplexy at the festival last night—during the raid. Blood is required to appease his spirit."

"Look out, Jimmy."

Cimarron's eyes darted to Cloud, who had shouted the warning.

Jumper stood immobilized as the other Seminoles all backed swiftly away from the rattlesnake that was winding its way through the low grass toward him.

"Shoot it," Cimarron barked to Wild Cat, but Wild Cat shook his head.

One of the other Seminoles said in a barely audible voice, "We dare not kill it. The power of its manes will hurt or kill us."

"What's manes?" Cimarron asked, his eyes on the sidewinder as it began to coil its body, its rattles whirring threateningly.

"Its spirit," the Seminole replied. "It will return and injure or kill the man who harms it."

Cimarron, as the rattlesnake drew back its raised head, thrust out his left arm and sent the immobilized Jumper sprawling backward. At the same instant, he drew his .44 and fired as the snake struck at the spot where Jumper had been standing only a moment before.

Blood spurted from the sidewinder's body and severed head. As its jaws gaped, its curved fangs were clearly visible. The body of the snake thrashed wildly. The eyes in its severed head gleamed and its forked tongue flickered.

"Stay away from its head," Cimarron ordered. "It can still bite."

Jumper rose slowly to his feet.

"Drop that gun," Wild Cat ordered Cimarron.

"No," Jumper said. "This deputy might have just saved my life. Keep an eye on him. But don't shoot him."

Cimarron holstered his gun.

"Shoot *them*," Jumper ordered. "It's time." He pointed to the three boys whose faces were frozen in fear.

"All of them?" Cloud asked.

"Sure, all of them," was Jumper's blunt reply. "Why not all of them?"

Cloud, frowning, said, "The Great Spirit allows a third of our enemies to be saved by lot. You know that, Jimmy."

"Sure, I know it, but it's not what the Great Spirit wants that counts right now. What counts right now is what I want, and what I want is to teach those damned vigilantes a lesson they're not likely to forget."

"I don't see why we have to kill them anyway," Black Dirt remarked hesitantly as he avoided looking directly at Jumper. "You said we'd just beat them up and then let them go."

"I changed my mind," Jumper snarled. "Beating them up's not going to appease the spirit of the old man the vigilantes scared to death last night. His spirit demands blood for blood. You all know that."

"We know it," Cloud agreed. "We also know that the Great Spirit says we must let one of these three live."

"All right," Jumper said with an angry gesture. "They can draw lots. We'll kill the two losers."

"*You'll* kill them," Mad Wolf said, speaking for the first time. "*We* won't. If there's to be any killing, you're the one who'll have to do it, Jimmy."

"Then I'll do it," Jumper stated emphatically as he bent down and broke off three blades of grass. He went over to the three seated boys, and holding out a fist from which grass blades sprouted, he said, "Pick one. Whoever gets the longest blade goes free."

"Let them go, Jumper," Cimarron said, "I've just come from talking to August Child. He's going to get the tribal

118

council to order the Lighthorsemen to hunt for the vigilantes. Me and you and your Red Sticks can help them hunt.''

Jumper ignored him. "Pick one!''

Hesitantly, one of the boys reached up, chose a blade of grass, and grinned as he saw how long it was. Just as hesitantly, the other two boys chose. When they realized that their companion's blade of grass was the longest of the three, they looked at each other in dismay. Then they looked at the stony-faced Jumper, who calmly drew his revolver and fired six shots into their bodies in rapid succession.

The two boys' bodies lurched soundlessly backward. One rolled a short distance and then came to a halt. The other, its throat torn apart, lay on its back where it had fallen, blood bubbling out of its bullet-shattered jugular vein.

Jumper gestured peremptorily, and the third boy, the one who had drawn the longest blade of grass, ran. Moments later, he disappeared into the trees that were some distance away.

Jumper smiled at Cimarron. "Watch out, Deputy." He pointed with his gun to the bloody head of the slain sidewinder. "That fellow's manes will be after you, and that means big trouble for you." His smile vanished, and then, looking over Cimarron's shoulder, he spoke several words in the Seminole language.

Wild Cat, standing behind Cimarron, raised his gun and brought it arcing swiftly downward. Its barrel struck the base of Cimarron's skull and sent him plunging down into a roaring blackness that was deeper than any night and devoid of everything except pain.

8

Fangs.

They loomed in front of Cimarron, menacing and seeming to be as long as swords. He tried to move away from them and found that he could not.

The sidewinder's mouth gaped wider, a lethal chasm. Its fangs glittered in the morning's sunlight. Its rattles whirred a warning.

Cimarron, hopelessly paralyzed, stared helplessly at the venomous fangs as the snake drew back its wedge of a head to strike . . .

His body suddenly convulsed as consciousness returned to him, banishing the nonexistent snake his nightmare had conjured. He found himself, as he got to his hands and knees, staring at the severed head, at the still-gaping mouth and fangs of the sidewinder he had shot earlier.

It's not your manes—your ghost—I've got to worry about, he thought as he reached for his hat, which had fallen off when he fell. It's the living I've got to be wary of, like Jumper and his Red Sticks. Not to mention that band of bastards who call themselves vigilantes.

He got unsteadily to his feet, and as he did so, pain rocketed in the spot where Wild Cat had struck him at the base of his skull. It radiated in waves throughout his head and neck. He stood stiffly, waiting for it to subside, and when it finally did, he gingerly felt the back of his head.

Blood.

He wiped his stained fingers on his jeans and walked slowly toward the trees in the distance and then in among them until he reached the place where his bay stood tethered. He climbed into the saddle, wincing at the pain the effort caused him, and then walked the horse north.

It was just before noon when he rode into Coonsville, where he asked directions to the Sloan ranch, and it was not long after noon when he arrived at the ranch. He asked the man repairing a pole corral where Sloan could be found.

"If you're looking for work," the man told him, "you're out of luck. Sloan's not hiring."

"It's not work I'm looking for, it's information. Now, would it put you out a whole lot to tell me where Sloan's to be found?"

"The house," the man said, pointing to it.

Cimarron went to it, dismounted, and knocked on the door.

"Yes?"

The man who had answered the door was robust and, Cimarron estimated, on one side or the other of fifty. "You Sloan?"

"I am. Who are you?"

Cimarron withdrew his badge from his pocket, displayed it, and said, "I'm a deputy marshal out of Fort Smith. Need some information about a man you know—Jimmy Jumper. He told me he was here to talk to you a while back. When was he here exactly?"

Sloan told him and Cimarron was neither surprised nor relieved that the man's answer seemed to indicate that Jumper had told the truth when he had said that he had been to see Sloan about August Child's tampering with the tribal accounts at the time that Clementine Jordan had been raped and murdered.

"What time of day did Jumper leave here?" Cimarron asked.

"He left the next morning. He stayed the night here."

"Much obliged, Sloan."

"Do you mind if I ask you why a deputy marshal such as yourself wants to know about Jimmy and his visit here?"

Cimarron told him. "Jumper's been accused of murder. But he told me he was here when the Jordan woman he's supposed to have killed was murdered, so it seems what he told me's the truth." As he swung into the saddle, Cimarron added, "He is, that is, if *you're* telling me the truth about him spending that particular night here at your place, Sloan."

"I have my vices," Sloan said stiffly, "but lying to lawmen's not among them."

Cimarron acknowledged the remark with a nod and then turned his bay and left Sloan behind him.

He sat loosely in the saddle as he rode south toward Wewoka, the muscles in his neck stiffening as he tried to hold his head in such a way as to relieve some of the pain. He wondered if Sloan had told him the truth about Jumper. He wondered if it were possible that Jumper had persuaded Sloan to lie and say that he had spent the night of Clementine Jordan's murder at the Sloan ranch.

But if Sloan's told me the truth, he thought as he ducked down over his horse's neck to avoid some low-hanging branches, then I'm left with one or two other questions. Like, if it wasn't Jimmy Jumper who killed Clementine Jordan, then who the hell was it? And if somebody else killed her, why'd Eunice go and claim that she'd seen Jumper—her faithful suitor, if not exactly her intended—do the deed?

He shook his head, more puzzled than ever, and the pain awoke and howled within his skull.

He consoled himself with the thought that he now knew things that might help him find out the answers to the two questions he had just asked himself. He reached into his pocket and withdrew the photographs he had obtained from Ken Andrews. He looked down at the one on top of the pile: the picture of the naked Clementine Jordan. He knew now that she had not lived the life of a straitlaced matron. That thought reminded him of Buster Schuyler's remark about Clay Jordan. Jordan, Schuyler had said, was so jealous of his wife that he wouldn't let another man come within a country mile of her.

But Andrews had said that Bennett, from whom he'd bought his photographs, had told him Clementine had had a lover. The pictures, Clementine had told Bennett, were a gift for her lover.

"Who was he?" Cimarron asked aloud, still staring at the photograph in his hand. "Who was your lover, lady?"

Clementine Jordan merely smiled coyly up at him.

Did your lover, whoever he was, murder you? he silently asked her. In a fit of jealousy maybe? Or maybe he was pestering you to leave your husband and run off with him, only you wouldn't and so he got mad at you and he . . .

His thoughts suddenly veered to Clay Jordan, and he recalled the social club's bar dog describing Clay Jordan's shocked and angry reaction to the photographs of his wife when Andrews had unwittingly shown them to him.

Had Clay Jordan confronted Clementine with his knowledge of the existence of the pictures, maybe killed her on account of them?

Jordan was a jealous man, the deputy thought. Buster Schuyler had testified to that fact. And these pictures—they could be reason enough for a jealous man to kill his wife for posing nude like that.

But it don't all fit together nice and neat, he thought. Mainly because Clay Jordan was in Coonsville the night his wife was murdered. At least, he'd said that's where he was. And Eunice told me she'd hid in the barn all night after the killing and hadn't come out till she'd seen her pa coming home in his wagon the next morning.

Well, I'll just have to have me another talk with Clay Jordan, he decided. And another one with Eunice, too. But first, since I'm a helluva lot closer to Wewoka than I am to Jordan's cabin, I'll go look up Elmer Bennett and have a word or two with him. If he's still in Wewoka after what the vigilantes did to him—and if he's still alive and kicking . . .

Maybe Bennett might be able to tell me who Clementine's lover was, since she mentioned she had one when she posed for her pictures. Bennett just might know something that'll help me catch whoever it was killed Clementine.

He pocketed the photographs and heeled the bay into a gallop despite the fact that the pounding rhythm of his riding caused his head to feel as if it were about to burst like an overripe melon left too long in the sun.

Some time later, Cimarron drew rein in front of Bennett's studio, dismounted, and tried the front door. Locked. He pounded on it, waited, then pounded on it again. No response. He turned, frustrated and annoyed, and found himself confronting a woman who looked vaguely familiar.

"Have you apprehended Jimmy Jumper?" she asked the deputy bluntly in a cold, rather piercing voice.

He recognized her as the woman who had been arguing with Elmer Bennett when he had ridden into town from the Jordan place with Reverend Forbes. Forbes had identified her as Wewoka's schoolmistress.

"Good day, Miss Pruitt," Cimarron said, touching the brim of his hat to her and thinking that, despite the ice in her voice, there was a fire in her eyes. Interesting.

"Well?"

"Well, what, Miss Pruitt?"

"Have you apprehended the man who murdered Clementine Jordan?"

"Nope."

"Then no woman in this town is safe from Jimmy Jumper."

"You're sure it was him who did the deed, are you?"

"Why, of course I am. Eunice saw him ra—saw what he did to her mother."

"So she told me."

"Why don't you send for reinforcements?"

"Reinforcements?"

"Other deputies . . . to help you apprehend that criminal."

"Doubt that I'll need any help."

"Do you? And yet Jimmy Jumper remains a free man."

"That's a fact, sad but true."

124

"Well, at least there are the vigilantes. I'm sure we can rely on them to rid us of that beast, even if the duly constituted authorities obviously cannot do so. I hope and I pray that Jumper will suffer severely for what he did to poor Clementine."

Vivian Pruitt turned away, misty-eyed. "Clementine was my dearest friend. She was so kind, so loving—a truly wonderful woman.

"I shall miss her sorely. We shared many good times together, Clementine and I." Vivian took a lace handkerchief from her reticule and dabbed at her wet eyes. "Would that I could have prevented the terrible wrongs that were done to her."

"I reckon her husband and daughter and the rest of her friends feel about the same way as you do, Miss Pruitt."

Vivian spun around to face Cimarron again. "I'm certain that Eunice and I and Clementine's other friends feel that way. But as for Clay Jordan, well, that, Deputy, may very well be quite another matter."

"What kind of another matter do you mean, Miss Pruitt?" Cimarron asked, his eyes narrowing as he studied Vivian's features tense with anger.

"Clay Jordan—if he'd been home with his family that night as he should have been, he could have protected Clementine from Jimmy Jumper's brutal attack. But no. He wasn't home. He was *there!*" Vivian pointed, her right arm stiff, her index finger quivering.

Cimarron looked in the direction she had pointed—at the social club. "Jordan was in there the night it happened? For how long?"

"I have no idea. But I know he was there. I happened to be passing and I saw him with my own two eyes."

Cimarron, his thoughts racing, was silent.

"I should think, Deputy, that you would be about the business of trying to apprehend Jimmy Jumper instead of trying to visit Mr. Bennett."

"I am about that very thing, Miss Pruitt."

"Are you, indeed?" Vivian's eyebrows rose. "Or are you

instead trying to buy some of Mr. Bennett's obscene photographs?''

''Nope. Couldn't buy any even if I wanted to, which I don't. The vigilantes burned them all up the night they blinded Bennett. I happened to be present when it happened.''

''I was relieved when I learned the next day what had happened—that Mr. Bennett would be able to take no more pictures of the obscene kind he was so fond of taking in the past.''

''I heard you and him arguing about the vigilantes here in town the other day. He was against them. You were on their side. So I'm not surprised you were all in favor of what the vigilantes went and did to him.''

''It was an admittedly extreme action and one that I find personally revolting, but, yes, I do endorse their having taken action against Mr. Bennett, even if I do not necessarily support the specific nature of that action. You must remember, Deputy, that harsh measures are required to destroy evil when it is discovered. I teach that personal maxim of mine to my pupils whenever the opportunity presents itself.''

''Do you happen to know where I might find Bennett?''

''I do not. Good day to you, Deputy.''

As Vivian Pruitt walked stiffly away from him, her head held high and the bustle on her dress bouncing jauntily, Cimarron made his way to the social club. Once inside it, he spoke to the bar dog, who was reading a newspaper. ''You told me about Elmer Bennett and Ken Andrews being in here one night, and about Bennett selling Andrews some of his photographs. As I recall it, you said Clay Jordan was in here the same night.''

''That's right. They were, and so was Clay.''

''What night was that exactly?''

The bar dog folded the newspaper, stared at the ceiling for a moment, and then said, ''It was a Tuesday.''

''Was it the same night that Jordan's wife was raped and murdered?''

''It was, yes. Why?''

Cimarron left the social club without bothering to answer

126

the bar dog's question. Jordan, he thought. The man told me he was in Coonsville the night his wife was killed. His daughter said he didn't show up until the next morning. But Miss Pruitt claims she saw him in the social club that night and the bar dog backs her up.

Something's out of whack somewhere. Maybe Jordan was on his way to Coonsville and stopped off at the social club on his way. Nope, that won't hold water; he'd have had to go pretty far out of his way to come to the social club. Coonsville's north of town. Well, I'll most certainly have to have that talk I've been planning with Jordan and his daughter.

Cimarron returned to Bennett's studio. He tried the door again. This time, it opened. He stepped inside. "Bennett?"

"Here."

Bennett's voice had come from the back room. Cimarron followed it.

"Who is it? Who's there?"

Cimarron identified himself and stood staring at the two puffy white bandages that covered the empty sockets where Bennett's eyes had once been. "I was here a little bit ago, Bennett, but you weren't."

"I was at the doctor's. Sit down, Cimarron. I'm glad you came. I've been wanting to talk to you, but rumor has it that you'd left town or been killed by the vigilantes."

"Rumor's wrong. What did you want to talk to me about, Bennett?" Cimarron sat down in a chair near Bennett's.

Bennett, his hands clasped on top of a cane he held in both hands, said, "I lied to you."

"You're not the first man—nor woman—who's done that, and I reckon you'll not be the last. What exactly did you lie to me about?"

"The photograph."

"What photograph?"

"I'm referring to the picture you showed me some days ago. The picture of the deputy the vigilantes crucified. I told you when you asked me about it that I hadn't taken it. That was a lie. I took it."

"And then you sent it off to the court in Fort Smith so

127

somebody would come here and find out about the vigilantes killing Cassidy. Somebody like me. Is that it?''

Bennett gripped his cane between his knees and his hands rose to touch the bandages covering his eye sockets. He shook his head. "I didn't send the picture to Fort Smith."

"Do you know who did?"

"No, not for sure. But I can tell you who hired me to take the picture. It was Eunice Jordan."

"Eunice Jordan! She got you to take that picture? Why?"

"I can tell you only what she told me. She told me that she wanted a picture of the man who had tried to protect Jimmy Jumper, who had raped and murdered her mother. She said she wanted to gloat over it—over what happened to him for his trouble. That was how she put it to me."

Cimarron leaned back in his chair. He thumbed his hat back on his head. "I'll be damned if I can figure this thing out. Bennett, do you think Eunice sent the picture to Fort Smith?"

"I don't know. I've wondered about that ever since you showed up here in Wewoka with it. I made only one print of it. She could have sent it. Or perhaps someone else managed to get their hands on it and send it.

"The point is, after what the vigilantes did to me, I made up my mind to tell you what I knew. I thought it might help you run down those bastards that blinded me."

Cimarron thought for a moment and then said, "Ken Andrews, before he died, told me you sold him some pictures you took of Clementine Jordan."

"So you know about them."

"Andrews told me that you'd told him that Mrs. Jordan wanted those pictures to give as a gift to her lover. Did she tell you who her lover was?"

Bennett shook his head. "I was in love with Clementine Jordan. But she wouldn't look twice in my direction. She came to me—I think to torment me—and said she wanted some nude pictures of herself. I agreed to take them. I thought that if I couldn't have her, I could at least make some extra prints and have them around to look at now and then. And then another idea suddenly occurred to me. I thought I could use them to blackmail her. I planned to threaten her with them, to say that I'd show them to her husband if she didn't let me know her carnally.

"She merely laughed at me. She said that if I ever dared let on that I'd taken such pictures of her, or if I ever showed them to anyone, she would say that I had forced her to pose for me. The vigilantes would hear about it, she said. She'd see to that. They'd defend her honor, she said. Her *'honor'* indeed! All this, remember, after she had just informed me that she had taken a lover.

"I sold prints of her pictures to that Andrews fellow when he drifted into town and—"

"Hold on a minute," Cimarron said, interrupting Bennett. "Weren't you taking a chance doing that? I mean, what if Andrews or somebody else recognized Mrs. Jordan? What if Andrews happened to show them to one of the men who make up the tribe of vigilantes or he told the man he had them?"

"I guess I was too drunk—and too mad at Clementine—to think straight at the time," Bennett answered. "All I could think about was getting revenge against her for spurning me. For me, selling her pictures to Andrews was, in a cockeyed kind of way, getting revenge on her. I liked to think of Andrews looking at her, thinking about her, having her—if only in his mind."

"You know what the vigilantes did to Andrews?"

"Yes, I heard about it."

"Andrews showed those pictures to a man who came into the social club after you'd left it that night. That man, as it turns out, was Clay Jordan."

Bennett's intake of breath was both sharp and sudden.

"Did you show those pictures to anybody else or tell anybody about them?"

When Bennett shook his head, Cimarron rose. "I'm obliged to you for finally leveling with me, Bennett. I hope you'll be feeling near to good as new before long."

129

Bennett lowered his head. "Once I'm through having to see the doctor here, I'm leaving town. I have no way now of making a living. I have a brother living up in Caldwell, Kansas. I wired him about my accident. He has asked me to come there and live with him and his family."

Bennett's voice faded. He lowered his head until his forehead was resting on the gnarled wood that topped his cane.

Cimarron recognized Reverend Forbes's surrey parked in front of the Jordan cabin as he rode up to it and dismounted. Leaving his bay with its reins trailing, he went up to the open door and was just about to knock on it when Forbes, who was inside the cabin, rose from his chair and reached out to touch Eunice. As his fingers brushed her body, Eunice, who had her back to the man, spun around and raised a hand to slap him. When she saw Cimarron standing in the doorway, she lowered her hand and then sat down in a chair by the table.

"Howdy, Eunice," Cimarron greeted her. "Forbes." As Forbes, a stricken expression on his face, turned toward the door, Cimarron asked, "Mind if I come in?"

Eunice frowned. Forbes managed a lopsided smile and then beckoned Cimarron inside.

"I was just visiting with Eunice," Forbes declared as Cimarron seated himself in an empty chair across from Eunice. "I'm afraid I've missed her father. Clay, Eunice tells me, is over at a neighbor's loading up a wagon with manure he intends to use to fertilize his field. It's nice to see you again, Cimarron."

"That Seminole festival, Reverend, turned out to be everything it was cracked up to be." Cimarron grinned.

Forbes's brow furrowed and his eyes sought the ceiling.

"You should have been there, Eunice," Cimarron remarked casually. "It was a whole lot more fun than a barn-raising."

"Scandalous," Forbes exclaimed, uttering the word as if it were a curse.

Cimarron pulled the picture of Cassidy from his pocket and tossed it on the table.

Forbes stared at it in horror for a moment before averting his eyes.

Eunice half-rose from her chair. Her hands shot up to cover her mouth. Her eyes darted to Cimarron's and then swiftly away. She sat down hard, her hands falling into her lap to lie there lifelessly.

"Reverend," Cimarron said, "Eunice has been trying to lend the law a hand where the murder of that deputy's concerned. That's right, isn't it, Eunice?"

"I don't know what you're talking about," she responded testily.

"Why, sure you do, honey," Cimarron insisted.

"Don't you 'honey' me, mister," Eunice cried. "Take that awful picture and go right on back wherever it is you just came from to act so big and bold and to tell lies about me."

"What is this all about, Cimarron?" Forbes asked, looking from Eunice to him.

"Reverend, why don't you tell Eunice there that the Good Book says she shouldn't be telling lies the way she's doing."

"Lies? What is he talking about, Eunice?"

"I don't know, and I don't want to know neither."

"Honey," Cimarron said, his voice bland, "I've just come from talking to Elmer Bennett and he told me you hired him to take that picture of Deputy Cassidy. He said you told him you wanted to gloat over it on account of Cassidy was trying to protect Jumper from the vigilantes even though Jumper killed your ma."

"That's not true," Eunice cried, shaking her head furiously.

"Eunice, dear," Forbes said, "to lie is a grievous sin in the eyes of the Lord."

"Did you send the picture to Fort Smith?" Cimarron shot at Eunice.

"No, it wasn't me who sent it! I—" She fell suddenly silent, alarm darkening her blue eyes.

"You say you didn't send it and in the saying you're admitting you knew about the picture," Cimarron pointed out. "Now, if you didn't send it, who did?"

"You're trying to mix me up," Eunice declared hotly. "I didn't say that. What I said was—"

"You had the only print of that picture—that print that's sitting right there on the table in front of you. Now, I'm going to ask you one more time, Eunice. Did you send it to Fort Smith?"

"Tell Cimarron the truth, Eunice," Forbes urged.

Eunice buried her face in her hands.

"You wanted to bring the murder of this poor man," Forbes continued, "to the attention of the authorities. Is that it, child?"

A low moan escaped Eunice's lips. She withdrew her hands from her face, threw back her head, and wailed wordlessly. "Yes!" she cried a moment later. "I paid Mr. Bennett to take it. Then I sent it to the law. But that's all I'm going to say. I'm not going to say another word more." She leaped to her feet and pointed to the door. "Now, get out, both of you, and don't neither of you ever come near me again. I don't need no preacher praying over me to save my immortal soul, nor do I need any scar-faced lawman with lust in his eyes leering at me! *Get out!*"

Forbes and Cimarron exchanged glances and then both men rose simultaneously and left the cabin.

"Cimarron, I'm not sure I understand any of what just transpired in there. Why did Eunice have that photograph taken by Bennett? Why did she send it to Fort Smith?"

"I'm not altogether sure of the answers to those questions myself, Reverend. But I have it in mind to try to find them out. Why don't you go on back to town? I'll try to calm Eunice down and see if I can't get to the bottom of this, since it's official business of mine."

Forbes nodded and climbed into his surrey. "I wish you good luck, Cimarron," he said before slapping the rump of his horse with his reins and driving away.

132

Cimarron squared his shoulders and strode back into the cabin.

"Get out!" Eunice screamed at him.

He didn't move, but stood with his eyes roving up and down her lithe and slender body. She flew at him, her fists striking his shoulders, his chest, and his shoulders again.

He seized her wrists and held her away from him. Her head tossed from side to side, her long brown hair flying first one way and then the other.

"Honey, simmer down some," he told her. "I'm not here to harm you. I'm here to help you if I can. But I can't help if you won't tell me what you did and why you did it—the truth."

Eunice dropped her head and leaned limply against him. "I can't," she wailed.

"Why can't you?" he asked, letting go of her wrists.

"Because I'm afraid," she moaned as his arms embraced her.

"What of?" He gently stroked her hair.

"The vigilantes and—" She fell silent.

"You lied to Bennett about why you wanted the picture of Cassidy's corpse. You didn't want it to gloat over like you told him. You wanted it to send to Fort Smith so that the court there'd send a lawman like me to find out who killed Cassidy."

When Eunice said nothing, Cimarron continued, "Jimmy Jumper says he wasn't around here the night your ma was murdered. He was staying the night with a rancher up north of Coonsville, name of Sloan. I talked to Sloan. He backed up Jumper's claim."

"I don't want to talk about Jimmy," Eunice stated flatly and firmly, looking up at Cimarron. "I want to talk about you. About the way you looked at me the first time you came here—" She placed her hands on his shoulders. "It was the same way you looked at me when Reverend Forbes was here just now."

133

"You were right, I reckon, about there being lust in my eyes."

"You were leering at me, too. Both times."

"I reckon you're right about that, too. I plead guilty on both counts. But there was what the law calls mitigating circumstances both times."

"I don't know what 'mitigating circumstances' means."

"Well, honey, in this case 'mitigating circumstances' means when a man like me meets a lovely young woman such as yourself he can't do a whole helluva lot to stop himself from lusting and leering."

"Jimmy's just a boy."

"I thought you didn't want to talk about him."

"But you—you're a man."

"You're right on that score, too."

"If I let you—you know—would you promise to stop asking me questions?"

Cimarron kissed her. He felt her lips part. He eased his tongue into her mouth and began to stiffen as she sucked on it. When their lips finally parted, he said, "I can't make you that kind of promise, honey." He kissed the tip of her pert nose. "I'm a lawman, and one of the things I got to do before I leave here is find out who killed your ma." He kissed her again—on the lips this time. His hands, flat on her back, pressed her body against his own. "You want to see justice done to whoever killed your ma." It was not a question. It was a flat statement.

"I want—"

Cimarron brought his right hand around Eunice's body and slid it into the bodice of her dress.

"—you."

"You can have me, honey. Any way you want me."

"Do you want me?"

"Do I?" Cimarron laughed heartily. "Oh, honey, now what kind of a question is that? Do I want you?" He laughed again. "Here. This'll answer your question for you." He took her right hand and placed it against his groin, where his erection was throbbing and threatening to burst through his jeans at any moment.

Eunice's hand tightened on it. "There's a room in the back."

Cimarron picked her up and carried her into it.

9

Cimarron gently placed Eunice down on the bed and then he sat down beside her and kissed her.

Her arms rose and encircled his neck.

He reached up, removed his hat, and dropped it on the floor. Easing closer to her, he opened the top buttons of her dress, beneath which she wore nothing. He gently fondled both of her breasts and then bent his head. His tongue slid from between his lips to touch and tease each of her nipples, which caused them to stiffen.

A moment later, he rose and said huskily, "Honey, let's you and me shuck our clothes and get on with it."

As he undressed, he watched Eunice pull her dress up over her head and toss it aside. Leaving his clothes and boots in a pile on the floor beside his hat, he lay down next to her and put his left arm around her, feeling the welcoming warmth of her body against his own as he did so.

She turned toward him and her right hand came to rest on his hip. Her left hand slithered under his neck and came to rest on the back of his head. She drew him toward her and kissed him with a fierceness that surprised him, but it confirmed, he thought, the fact that she wanted him.

He reached down and raised her right leg slightly, letting his shaft settle between her thighs. Then, releasing her leg, he drew her closer to him, exulting as the two soft mounds of her breasts pressed hotly against his chest.

Her kisses landed indiscriminately on his cheeks, chin, nose, lips. She caressed his back, sending exciting sensations shivering through him.

He eased her over on her back and then straddled her, supporting himself on his hands and knees as he gazed down into the depths of her wide-open blue eyes. And then her eyes lowered to his erection, which was slanting downward toward her navel, and she reached out and took it in both of her hands. She stroked it lightly and then looked up at him. Her lips parted. She looked down again.

Cimarron eased forward, accepting her wordless invitation, and as he did so, Eunice's tongue darted from between her lips to touch the tip of his erection. He shuddered as her tongue swirled sensuously and the head of his shaft began to glisten wetly as a result of her ministrations. She closed her lips, kissed his erection, and then pressed against his shoulders. He eased his body backward and Eunice seized him and began to guide him into her.

He sank eagerly into her steamy wetness, and as she as eagerly fitted herself to him, he began to buck, slowly at first and then more rapidly, feeling her answering lunges and aware of her little cries of ecstasy as her arms and then her legs embraced him.

He slowed the pace of his thrusting, his head buried in her hair, which splayed out over the pillow. When he felt her convulse and heard her cry out, he plunged downward until all of him was within her. As her fingernails bit into his back, his hips rose and fell, rose and fell.

The world slipped away from him and he felt himself riding a soaring tide that surged ever upward toward the crest he knew was coming. But he held himself back until Eunice beneath him cried out again and then clawed his back as she attained a second orgasm. Only then did he begin to buck in earnest, his loins slapping hard against Eunice's as sweat bathed both of their bodies and the heady scent of sex filled his nostrils.

As he plunged into her as far as he could go, he exploded, and Eunice cried out his name as he flooded her.

"Oh, honey," he murmured, nuzzling her neck as his body finally stilled and the world slowly returned to him. "Honey, that was—"

"Wonderful!" she murmured.

"Wonderful," he repeated as she stirred lazily beneath him and then stretched languidly.

He withdrew from her and she curled up beside him, her head nestled against his chest. He ran a finger along the lines of her eyebrows and then brushed some stray strands of hair from her forehead.

"I'm not afraid now," she whispered in his ear. "Not with you here, I'm not."

"What's there to be afraid of, honey?" he asked as casually as he could, hoping Eunice might decide to tell him more than she had earlier.

"I told you, the vigilantes. If they knew I sent that picture of Deputy Cassidy to the court . . ." She buried her face against Cimarron's chest and, in a childlike gesture, used both hands to shield her already hidden eyes.

Then she drew back and looked anxiously at Cimarron.

"You won't tell them, will you?"

"Nope. I won't tell anybody. Is it just the vigilantes you're fearing, honey?"

"What do you mean?"

"Well, I thought you might be afraid Jumper might come back here and raise some kind of ruckus with you like he did before with your ma."

"Jimmy wouldn't do that."

"You're certain about that, are you?"

Eunice ran a finger around the perimeter of Cimarron's right nipple. "I'm sure."

"I've heard people say that killers always return to the scene of their crime."

"Jimmy and I—we never did what you and me just done. I told him I wouldn't till we got married. Did you know he wants to marry me?"

"You mentioned something about it the first time we met. You also came close to admitting to me before that you're still in love with him despite what he went and done to your ma."

"I know I did. But the plain truth of the matter is that I don't really know whether I'm in love with him or not. He's come courting me now for near to a year, and sometimes it seemed like I was *supposed* to be in love with him. He'd gotten to be a habit with me. Like taking a bath every Saturday night. But I think now that what I want isn't him so much as it is a big strapping man like you. Jimmy's such a skinny little thing."

"Not to mention the fact that he's a murderer. You did the right thing sending that picture to Fort Smith. I'm bound and determined to run Jumper to ground for killing your ma. And when I do, he'll hang."

Cimarron felt Eunice stiffen. "Hanging's a hard way for a man to die," he added solemnly. When she withdrew from him and turned over on her back to stare up at the ceiling, he continued, "I've seen cases where the rope didn't break hanged men's necks. It took them as long as ten minutes to finally die. They choked to death. Like I said, hanging's a mighty hard way for a man to have to die.

"But you did the right thing, honey, there's no doubt about that. Jumper's got to pay the price for what he done to your ma." Cimarron propped himself up on one elbow and looked down at Eunice.

A tear trickled from her left eye and rolled down her cheek. "Jimmy didn't do it," she said softly, closing her eyes.

"You trying to tell me it wasn't Jumper who killed your ma?"

"Yes. He wasn't the one who killed her."

"But, honey, you told everybody it was him. You told everybody you saw him do it. You told *me* you saw him rape and then kill your ma,"

"I lied."

Cimarron heard the echo of Elmer Bennett saying the same

thing to him not long ago. "Did you lie about being here the night your ma was killed, too?"

"I was here." A tear oozed out from under Eunice's right eye, hovered a moment, and then slid down her cheek. "I didn't lie about that. I saw what happened to Ma." She covered her hands with her face and began to sob.

Cimarron embraced her and held her close to him until she finally stopped crying.

"I wanted to tell the truth from the start," Eunice cried. "I did. I really truly did. Only I *couldn't!*"

"Why not?"

"Will you take me away with you if I tell you the truth now? Will you take me someplace where it's safe and hide me?"

"Sure, I will, honey. You can count on it. Now, tell me. Who'd you see kill your ma?"

Eunice sat up in the bed. She wrapped her arms around her naked body and sat there, not looking at Cimarron, soundlessly shaking her head.

"You won't tell me?" He also sat up. As he put his arm around Eunice's shoulders, she jumped from the bed and hurriedly slipped her dress over her head and her shoes on her feet. "I can't tell you," she exclaimed, and ran from the room.

Cimarron rose. He dressed, strapped on his cartridge belt, and then went into the main room of the cabin, where he found Eunice at the stove, her back to him.

"Sit down," she said. "I'm fixing us some supper. You hungry?"

I'm hungry for information, he thought, but he said, "I'm starved. I'm so hungry, in fact, I could bite the bark off a tree." He sat down at the wooden table, his eyes on Eunice's back as she stirred the contents of an iron skillet, wondering how to go about finding out from her what he wanted—needed—to know.

When she turned, stony-faced, toward him, the skillet in one hand and a large two-tined fork in the other, he decided now was not the time. He was sure she would refuse to

140

answer him just as she had refused to do so only moments ago. He noted the firm set of her jaw and her compressed lips as she forked fried potatoes mixed with onions onto a plate and set it in front of him.

She handed him a fork, and despite its bent tines, he was able to use it. He chewed the too-salty food and then, after swallowing, said, "How'd you like to pay a visit to Fort Smith?"

She glanced at him from her place across the table, where she was using a spoon to push crisped potatoes and onions from one side of her plate to the other. "Go all the way to Arkansas?"

"Fort Smith's not all that far from here. I figure you could stay there until I find out who really killed your ma. Once I do, then you could come back here and not have a thing to worry about anymore."

"Pa—" Eunice seemed to have had difficulty uttering the word. "Pa'd tan my hide, were I to leave here to go someplace else."

"No, he wouldn't. Not if you didn't tell him you were going, he wouldn't. You'd be safe in Fort Smith."

"Safe," Eunice echoed. She sighed, shook her head. "He'd find me. Somehow he would. I know he would."

"Who? Your pa, you mean?"

Eunice looked down at the uneaten food on her plate.

"Then who'd find you?" Suddenly Cimarron understood. "You mean the man who killed your ma?"

Eunice nodded.

He reached across the table, took her free hand, and squeezed it. "If I could catch him, you'd be safe for sure and certain. And, honey, you can help me catch him. You know that. All you got to do is give me his name and tell me where you think I might be able to run him to ground."

Eunice pulled her hand free and stood up so suddenly that she upended the chair on which she had been sitting and it crashed to the floor.

Cimarron, thinking he had pressed her too hard and had

frightened her badly as a result, started to rise and reach for her when a male voice muttered, "Sit down, Deputy!"

His eyes swung around to the open door behind him. He found himself staring into the muzzle of a shotgun the vigilante, who was robed and hooded, was aiming at him.

There was the sudden sound of something tearing and he turned again to see the barrel of another rifle thrust through the greased butcher paper that had covered the window. He slowly sat down.

The vigilante in the doorway stepped forward and held out one hand. Cimarron pretended not to understand the peremptory gesture.

"Give it to me—your gun!" the hooded man said sharply.

Cimarron reluctantly handed over his revolver, which the vigilante promptly slid through a slit in his robe and placed in his waistband. As he withdrew his hand, the gun bulged beneath his black robe.

"No," Eunice whispered, and backed up against the wall. "Oh, dear God, *no!*"

"Let's go," the vigilante facing Cimarron said, and began to back out of the room.

Cimarron rose and followed him out of the cabin, not at all surprised to find five more robed and masked vigilantes waiting outside in the night, all of them armed with revolvers. As the one who had thrust his rifle through the cabin window joined the others, Cimarron thought, seven of them against the one of me.

"You come on out here, girl," shouted the vigilante who had been in the cabin. Cimarron realized the man was speaking in oddly guttural tones.

He's trying to disguise his voice, he thought. That means either me or Eunice or maybe both of us probably knows his voice—knows him. "Leave her be," he told the man. "It's me you want."

"You're but half-right," the vigilante snarled. "We want her, too. Eunice has a bad habit of interfering with other folks' business."

As Eunice timidly emerged from the cabin, the man turned

142

to her and said, "You never should have sent that picture of the dead deputy to the law, girl."

"Cimarron," Eunice cried, "you told them!"

"Not me, honey," he said quickly. "I didn't tell anybody, and that's the truth."

"Then how—how did you find out?" Eunice asked the vigilante with the shotgun.

"Deputy," the man said, ignoring Eunice's question, "you and the girl get up on your horse."

Cimarron hesitated a moment and then held out his hand to Eunice.

She shrank from him.

He took a step toward her and gripped her wrist. "We've got to do like they say," he whispered to her. "We don't, and they're likely to shoot us down like dogs right here where we stand. We've got to go with them. But maybe we'll come out of this all right yet. Come on, honey."

He led her to his bay, climbed aboard the animal, and then helped her up behind him.

"Follow me," the vigilante ordered as he and his companions mounted their horses.

Cimarron moved the bay out behind the gray gelding the vigilante with the shotgun was riding, and as he did so, Eunice's arms encircled his body.

She held tightly to him during the silent ride through the equally silent night. But later, as the sound of laughter from the vigilantes riding behind them broke the stillness, her embrace grew even tighter, a clear indication of her fear.

"Where are they taking us?" she asked Cimarron.

"I'm not sure, but I can guess."

"Where?"

"To where they crucified Cassidy."

Eunice gasped. And then, "They're going to crucify us, too?"

"Hush, honey," he admonished, not wanting to answer her question. "I got to think. Find us a way out of this fix we're in."

Eunice remained mute throughout the rest of the journey,

but as they rode out of a grove of shin oaks and she saw the crossed planks on which Cassidy had died, she screamed, a shrill piercing sound that shattered the quiet night and sent unseen birds fluttering frantically through the branches of the tall trees.

"Shut your goddamned mouth, girl," the vigilante leading the procession barked.

But Eunice, instead of obeying the man's order, screamed a second time.

One of the vigilantes who was riding in the rear suddenly galloped up to her, seized her by the hair, and threw her to the ground. "You heard the man," he muttered. "One more peep out of you and it'll be your last!"

Cimarron looked down at the spot where Eunice lay silent and cringing and then up at the crossed planks not far away that were stained with dried blood.

"Take a good look, Deputy," said the vigilante with the shotgun. "You came to Wewoka to find out what happened to Cassidy and now you're going to find out more than you wanted to know. Like what he felt like while he was nailed to those planks before we shot him. But before we nail you up there, we're going to teach the girl a lesson she won't soon forget, and you're welcome to watch her learn." The man gestured and one of the other vigilantes hauled Eunice to her feet.

"Gag her," the leader of the group ordered when she began to scream again, and one of the vigilantes immediately did so.

Another dismounted, removed a rope from his saddle horn, and then, with the help of a third man, wrapped the struggling Eunice's arms around the thick trunk of a tree and tied her wrists together.

Cimarron turned and saw the leather bullwhip in the hands of a vigilante who was snaking it out into the air and causing it to crack ominously.

Eunice turned her head, and when she saw the bullwhip, she began to struggle in a fruitless attempt to free herself.

"You got any notions about helping the girl, Deputy,"

144

said the still-mounted man holding the shotgun, ''and you'd best get shut of them real fast. If you move, I'll shoot you. You ever seen a man who's been shot with this here kind of gun?''

Cimarron had. An image of a blasted body, ripped literally to shreds when fired upon by a man with a shotgun at close range flashed through his mind, an image of fire belching from the barrel of the gun, an image of bloody flesh and broken bones flying through the air.

Thwappp!

Cimarron turned his head just in time to see the bullwhip wrap itself around Eunice's body and the tree to which she was tied. He stared, his body stiff and his teeth grinding together, as the whip was withdrawn and the man drew it back and . . .

Thwappp!

Eunice's dress split in a horizontal line just below her shoulders as a result of the second blow, and Cimarron saw a thin line of blood form on her bare back where the leather had landed. As the man with the whip prepared to strike a third time, Cimarron lunged to one side. He ducked down under the belly of one of the vigilantes' horses and came up running on the other side of the animal, heading toward the man with the whip.

The man turned, startled, toward him. He raised the whip high above his head, intending to bring it down on Cimarron. But Cimarron sprinted even faster, and when he reached the man, he seized his wrist and wrenched the whip out of his hand. He turned, whirling the whip around above his head, indiscriminately striking both men and horses unlucky enough to be within the range of the whip's wide arc.

A horse screamed and reared, throwing its rider.

A man cursed as his black hood was almost torn from his head.

The vigilante with the shotgun fired but missed Cimarron, who had leapt onto the back of the riderless mount and, still swinging the whip, headed toward the man who had just fired at him.

But before he reached the man, the woods in the distance suddenly erupted with sound and motion.

The leader of the vigilantes spurred his horse and the animal dashed away from Cimarron, who turned to see a number of riders bearing swiftly down upon the vigilantes. And then, as they came closer, he recognized the man leading them—Jimmy Jumper.

Jumper was brandishing his revolver above his head and whooping at the top of his voice.

That's Cloud, Cimarron thought, recognizing the man behind Jumper. And that's Black Dirt and Mad Wolf over there. There's Wild Cat, too. The others he did not recognize.

The vigilantes scattered before the unexpected onslaught, firing at the Red Sticks who were firing at them.

One of the vigilantes—Cimarron was sure it was the one who had been wielding the whip—tried to climb aboard the horse being ridden by one of his companions, but a Red Stick bullet struck him in the back and he lost his grip on the saddle's cantle and on his shotgun and fell to the ground.

Jumper whooped and, grinning, put another bullet in the fallen man's back, causing his body to lurch and his hands to claw the ground convulsively.

Cimarron lashed out with the whip in his hand, but he missed the vigilante he had been aiming at, hitting instead the rump of the man's mount and causing it to race, screaming, away.

More shots were fired by both the vigilantes and the Red Sticks, causing fire to flash and smoke to stream from gun barrels.

Cimarron caught a glimpse of Black Dirt as the man flew over his horse's neck when the animal took several shots in the withers, which killed the horse in midstride and caused it to fall clumsily to the ground. As Black Dirt hurtled to the ground and rolled over, Cimarron heeled the vigilante's mount under him and rode swiftly toward Eunice. Before he reached her, he leapt from the saddle and the horse he had been riding went galloping into the trees.

He quickly untied her wrists and then he removed the gag

from her mouth and threw it on the ground. He held her close to him as he stood with his back pressed against the tree to which she had been bound. The shooting beyond it continued.

He wasn't sure how much time had passed when the shooting finally ended and only the strong smell of gunsmoke bore testimony to what had passed. The body of the leader of the vigilantes, who had been shot twice in the back—once by Jumper—now lay facedown and unmoving on the grass, his black robe crumpled in folds about his bent knees.

"You stay here, honey," he told Eunice.

But she clutched at his arm and pleaded, "Don't leave me. *Please!*"

"You'll be fine. I'll be right back. Stay out of sight—back there behind that tree."

When she had placed herself behind the tree, he headed for the vigilante lying on the ground. But before he reached the man, Jumper rode up to him, drew rein, and said, "This makes us even, Deputy. You saved my ass from that sidewinder and now I've saved your ass from whatever it was those bastards had planned for it."

"That's right, Jumper. We're even now."

"Go after them," Jumper shouted to his Red Sticks.

"How'd you happen to show up here?" Cimarron asked him as Black Dirt got up behind the cantle of Cloud's saddle and the pair rode with the other Red Sticks into the woods in search of the fleeing vigilantes.

"Heard screams," Jumper answered. "We were camped on the southern edge of those woods over there. We came to investigate. Is Eunice all right?"

"She's hurt some, but I reckon she'll be all right. She told me you didn't kill her ma, that she had lied about that. Maybe you can get her to tell you who did do it. I've not been able to get her to name the man—at least, not so far, I haven't."

"I can't stop to talk to her now. I've got some vigilantes to catch."

"Jumper—"

Cimarron's words were lost as Jumper gave an eager whoop

147

and rode off into the night after his Red Sticks. Cimarron made his way toward the downed vigilante.

"Wait for me," Eunice cried.

He halted, and then, when Eunice had joined him and nervously taken his hand in hers, he walked on. When he reached the man lying on the ground, he put out a boot and turned him over on his back.

The man groaned. His fingers twitched.

Cimarron pulled the man's robe up around his waist and then removed his own .44 from the man's waistband. "Take his hood off, honey."

Eunice released her hold on Cimarron's hand. She took a step toward the man and then a step backward.

"It's all right," Cimarron told her. "If he tries anything, I'll see to it that a third bullet joins up with the two he's already got inside him."

Eunice stepped forward, bent down, reached out, hesitated, and then quickly snatched the hood from the man's head. She gasped and stepped back to stand beside Cimarron, both of her hands clutching his right arm as she stared down at the face of the man that was bathed in moonlight.

"Help," the man murmured, trying and failing to open his eyes.

"You're past being helped," Cimarron told him bluntly.

"Get doctor," sighed the Reverend Omar Forbes. Then his eyes opened to stare glassily up at Cimarron and his hand slid slowly along the ground. Moments later, his fingers clutched Cimarron's left boot. "Doctor," he repeated.

"You," Eunice muttered, her grip tightening on Cimarron's arm as she stared down at the obviously dying preacher. "You had them flog me! You were going to crucify Cimarron!" She suddenly let go of Cimarron's arm and kicked out savagely. Her shoe buried itself in Forbes' fleshy body, and he released his hold on Cimarron's boot. As she drew back her foot to kick him a second time, Cimarron pulled her away.

"Let me go," she cried, struggling to free herself. "I'll kick him to death, the son of a bitch!"

"You'll not. Now, settle yourself down." Turning his

148

attention from Eunice to Forbes, Cimarron asked, "Why, Reverend?"

"Sin," Forbes hissed. "Everywhere—sin and sinners sinning." The sibilance of his words was followed by bubbles of blood that grew like a bright-red fungus from between his lips, a fungus that bloomed and then burst.

"Wanted to teach"—Forbes coughed and bloody strings of saliva flew from his mouth—"righteousness."

"Righteousness," Eunice cried. She began to laugh hysterically. "He wanted to teach the rest of us righteousness," she shouted, her head thrown back in manic glee. "Cimarron, this son of a bitch felt me up more times than I could keep track of. He did! Here!" she cried, her hands cupping both of her breasts. "Here!" Her hands clapped hard against her buttocks. "*Here!*" she screamed, her hands coming to nest between her legs.

"All the time he kept coming to the cabin and talking Bible talk, but when my pa wasn't there, he was all the time slobbering over me, pawing me—"

Cimarron pulled Eunice back as she tried again to kick Forbes.

As if he had heard none of what Eunice had said, Forbes murmured, "Must stamp out sin. Show sinners paths of righteousness."

"Shut up and listen to me, Forbes," Cimarron snapped as he got down on one knee beside the dying man. "Who rode with you? I want their names. Every last one of them."

"Angels of instruction," Forbes whispered.

"Devils of destruction is what you mean," Cimarron snarled impatiently. "Now, who the hell are they—those men you were leading tonight and all those other times?"

"As it is written, 'there is none righteous, no, not one,' " Forbes quoted from the Bible, and then added in a tremulous tone, "Not even me, thy poor servant, Lord."

Cimarron seized him by the shoulders and shook him. "Who are the vigilantes? Name them to me, Forbes! Every man jack of them!"

Forbes suddenly pushed Cimarron away from him with

surprising strength. He sat up, his body stiff, and when he spoke his Biblical words again, his voice was strong, a clarion call: " 'Yea, the light of the wicked shall be put out and the spark of his fire shall not shine.' "

Forbes's body slumped down upon the ground.

Eunice peered down at him through wide eyes. "Is he . . ."

Cimarron placed the first two fingers of his right hand against the side of the man's neck and found no pulse. He rose. "He's dead."

"I hope he burns in hellfire forever," Eunice muttered from between her clenched teeth.

"I reckon he will if the Lord's got the good sense most folks give Him credit for."

"Cimarron?" He turned to face Eunice. "How do you suppose the vigilantes knew?"

"Knew?"

"That I sent Deputy Cassidy's picture to Fort Smith."

"That's easy enough to answer. The preacher there, he was visiting you when I arrived. I made the bad mistake of questioning you about that picture in front of him and you made the worse mistake of admitting in front of him that it was you who sent it to Judge Parker's court. That's how he found out about what you'd done. When he left, he wasted no time rounding up his boys and coming back after you—and me."

Cimarron looked around, and when he saw his bay quietly grazing in the distance, he holstered his gun, took Eunice by the hand, and led her toward the animal.

"I guess we're lucky," Eunice mused, "If Jimmy hadn't of come when he did . . ." Her words trailed away. And then, "Did he say anything about me?"

"Just that he didn't have time to talk to you. His blood was up and he was hell-bent on riding out after the rest of those vigilantes."

"I'll thank him for his trouble next time I see him."

When they reached the bay, Eunice looked up at Cimarron. "What am I to do now? I can't go home. They might come after me again. But I don't know where I *can* go."

Cimarron stood, one hand on his saddle horn, thinking about what Eunice had said. "You're right as rain about not being able to head back home. There's the hotel in town—no, that's no good." He looked at Eunice, at her tearstained face and frightened eyes. "You got any good friends in town you could hole up with till things quiet down?".

She slowly and sadly shook her head. "Pa hardly ever let me go to town once I'd finished my schooling there."

Schooling.

Cimarron grinned. "I got a place I can put you where you'll be safe and sound."

"Where? What place?"

He answered her questions and then climbed into the saddle and helped her up behind him. He heeled the bay and they rode south toward Wewoka.

10

Cimarron came up on the house from behind in order to avoid being seen riding down the street.

He dismounted and helped Eunice to the ground. As he was wrapping his reins around one of the two slender poles that supported the small overhang above the back door, he said, "Miss Pruitt'll be glad to give you shelter, or I miss my guess. She told me she was a real good friend of your ma's and I reckon of yours, too, since she must have been your teacher when you were in school."

"Yes, she was my teacher and she was always real nice to me, almost as nice as she always was to Ma."

"So you'll be safe with her."

"But what if she finds out that the vigilantes are after me? If she does find out, maybe she'll be too scared to let me stay with her."

"Stop your fretting, honey, and let's have a talk with her. There's just no use in worrying that the bridge you want to cross might be burned down or washed away by the time you get to it." Cimarron looked up at the lighted window on the second floor above the overhang. "Once we're inside, we'll have us a look at where you're hurt and see what we can do about it. We'll fix you up fine." He knocked lightly on the door and waited. When there was no response, he knocked again, more loudly this time.

Moments later, the door was opened by Vivian Pruitt, who held a lamp in her hand.

"Eunice!" she exclaimed. "Whatever are you doing here at this time of night?" She glanced at Cimarron. "What's wrong? What's happened?"

"I'd be much obliged to you, Miss Pruitt, if you'd let us step inside."

"Oh, of course. Come in, both of you."

When they were inside the kitchen, Vivian placed the lamp on a table, and then, as Eunice slumped down into one of the chairs beside it, she exclaimed, "My dear, you've been hurt!" Her eyes impaled Cimarron. "Did you do that to her?" She pointed to the two whip wounds that were now crusted with dried blood.

"Nope. It was—"

"A vigilante did it," Eunice interrupted. "The bastard," she added angrily.

"Eunice," Vivian exclaimed, her face coloring. "Such language. A vigilante, you say?"

Cimarron told her what had happened and concluded by saying, "Since you and Mrs. Jordan were such good friends, I thought you might not mind if Eunice stayed here with you for a spell. She'll be safe here. Once I've got my hands on the rest of those vigilantes, she can go on back home and pick up her regular life where it's been left off."

"Reverend Forbes is dead, you say," Vivian murmured as she clasped and unclasped her hands nervously. "How simply terrible!"

"What about it, Miss Pruitt?" Cimarron prodded.

"What about what? Oh, Eunice. Yes, of course she is most welcome to remain here with me. I'll be only too glad to look out for her. But, Deputy, do you really think you can catch those vigilantes?"

"I'll catch them, sooner or later, one way or another."

"I must say that you do sound confident. Forgive me, but you also sound rather arrogant."

"Don't mean to sound arrogant. It's just that I'm bound and determined to get my hands on them."

Vivian cupped Eunice's chin in one hand and raised her head. Smiling down into the young woman's upturned face, she said, "My, but you do bear quite a striking resemblance to your dear departed mother. Clementine was, as you are, Eunice, quite an attractive woman." Vivian withdrew her hand and stepped behind Eunice. "Oh, just look at what those beasts have done to you, you poor thing! I shall go at once and fetch the doctor."

"I doubt that there's any real need for you to do that, Miss Pruitt," Cimarron remarked. "If you can just heat up some water and get me some clean cloths, I'll wash and bind up Eunice's wounds."

"But—but there is the very real danger of infection. Really, Deputy, I think Eunice should have the attention of a doctor in this case."

Cimarron shrugged. "It can't hurt, I reckon."

"I'll be but a few minutes. The doctor lives only a few blocks from here. Excuse me, please. I'll return just as soon as I possibly can." Vivian hurried out of the kitchen, and a moment later Cimarron heard the front door open and then close.

"That's odd, now, isn't it?" he asked idly, stroking his chin.

"What's odd?"

"The lady was all dressed up when she let us in, just as if she'd been expecting company this late at night."

"It's not odd a'tall," Eunice insisted. "She had to get dressed before she could open the door to whoever she might find outside. She couldn't do it in her nightdress, now, could she?"

Cimarron grinned at Eunice. "Maybe Miss Pruitt couldn't, but I confess I've known a woman or two in my time who'd go and do that very thing—especially if it was me they were expecting might come by."

Still thoughtfully stroking his chin, he continued, "Now, why do you suppose she didn't blink an eye when I told her Reverend Forbes was a vigilante?"

"All she could think of, probably, was that he was dead.

154

She was a churchgoing woman, my ma always said, and I guess she was shocked to hear that her preacher got himself killed, never mind how or who he really was on the sly."

Cimarron went around behind Eunice and stared down at the welts on her back. "They're not all that deep," he commented. "They'll like as not not need sewing up."

"Cimarron, I've made up my mind."

He went around to the other side of the table and sat down facing Eunice. "You've made up your mind about what?"

"To tell you. What you want to know. What you've been pestering me about."

"Tell me, then."

"First, you've got to promise me something. Will you?"

"Maybe. Maybe not. It depends on what you want me to promise you."

"I want you to promise me you won't let him hurt me."

"You mean the man who murdered your ma?"

"You promise to protect me from him? Cross your heart and hope to die if you don't?"

Cimarron suppressed a smile. "I cross my heart." He did. "And hope to die if I don't protect you from—from who, Eunice?"

She hesitated, looked down at the table. She looked up at Cimarron as if she were seeking some further assurance that he was capable of protecting her. He reached across the table and took her hands in his.

"My pa."

Cimarron's hands tightened on hers. "Did I hear you right?" he asked soberly. "You're telling me it was your daddy who killed your ma?"

Eunice nodded, her eyes cast down again.

"You're sure?"

"I saw him do it."

"Then what you told me the day I first talked to you about what happened—"

"Most of what I told you was true. But it wasn't Jimmy who killed Ma; it was Pa. What really happened—I was home with Ma that night, and then Pa came home and he was boiling mad and said he'd just come from town, where he'd found out that Ma had had Mr. Bennet take some pictures of her and he'd just seen them. He said they were dirty pictures, and Ma, she just laughed, but I could tell she was scared stiff, and then Pa asked her why she'd gone and done what she did.

"She acted real brave, but her eyes looked leery of what Pa might have in mind to do to her. She said she'd had them taken to give to somebody she loved. I thought, when she said that, that Pa was going to explode. His face, it got all red and there was this vein in his forehead—I could see it bulging out like it was about ready to pop. He hit her. He wanted to know who they were for—the pictures—but Ma wouldn't tell him.

"He hit her again. And then again." Eunice sobbed.

Cimarron's hand rose and gently stroked her cheek. As he did so, her hot tears wet his fingers.

Drawing a deep breath, Eunice continued, "I tried to make Pa stop, but he wouldn't. He kept hitting her and then he started tearing at her clothes. He said if she wanted loving, well, he was all set to give her some. I tried to stop him, but there just wasn't any stopping him. He opened his pants and he was—well, ready—and he threw Ma down on the floor and climbed on top of her. Oh, it was so awful, what with her screaming and him grunting! I couldn't stand it. I ran out of the house and just stood outside, trying to think what to do. Ma, she kept on screaming. I put my hands over my ears, but I could still hear her. So I ran to the barn and I hid in the hayloft. Pretty soon Ma got quiet. I thought it was all over. But it wasn't.

"She made this terrible loud noise—not a scream. It was like the way hogs squeal when their throats get cut at slaughtering time. It sounded close. Real close. I couldn't help myself. I had to see what— I climbed down from the hayloft and ran to the barn door. Pa, he had his butchering knife and he kept stabbing Ma. She wasn't making any more noise by then. She was on the ground. Just there—on the ground. Not fighting back. Not moving at all. That's when I knew for sure that she was gone.

"Pa, he was panting the way he does after he's done digging out a tree stump or after he's hauled a real heavy load of logs out of the woods. His pants, they were still open, and Ma . . . what clothes she still had on were all bloody, and so were Pa's pants.

"He looked up and saw me. He started for me. I ran, but he caught me. He said did I see what he'd done. I told him I did. He said if I told a living soul about it, he'd kill me like he'd just killed Ma. I knew he would. He wasn't right in the head anymore, it seemed to me. His eyes, they were wild, like he had a fever or something."

When Eunice fell silent, Cimarron said, "You promised you wouldn't tell on him."

Eunice nodded. "Then he said we'd blame it on Jimmy, say that Jimmy did it. He told me what to tell folks. He told me over and over again what to tell them."

Cimarron recalled listening to Eunice the time she had described her mother's rape and murder to him. He recalled thinking that she had sounded then as if she were reciting a lesson she had learned by rote. That's exactly what she was doing, he thought.

Eunice looked up at him. He gently brushed the tears from her cheeks.

"So now you know why I was so fearful of telling you."

"Don't blame you one bit for being fearful, honey. But you don't have to be that way now. I'll take care of you." He rose, and as he started for the door, Eunice, her eyes wide, also rose.

"You're not leaving, are you?"

He turned back to her. "Forbes said, when he was at your cabin before, that your daddy was over at a neighbor's place loading up a wagon with manure."

"That's where Pa said he was going, yes."

"What neighbor's place? Tell me how to find it."

"You're going there after him?"

"I expect he'll be to home by now. But if I don't find him at your cabin, my next stop'll be at your neighbor's place."

Eunice told him what he wanted to know. "Couldn't you wait till daylight to leave?"

Cimarron crossed the room and placed his palms on her cheeks. "You're safe here for the time being. You'll be still safer once I've got your pa put away. I'll be back to see you as soon as I've done that." He bent down and kissed her forehead.

A moment later, he was outside the house and freeing his bay. He stepped into the saddle, turned the horse, and rode away from the house.

I was about on target, he thought. Once I was pretty sure that Jumper didn't do it, on account of Sloan backing up his story, I figured the finger pointed straight at Jordan on account of him having been in the social club the night of the killing instead of up in Coonsville like he'd told everybody, including me. He made that Coonsville story up out of whole cloth to cover himself, and nobody had bothered or cared enough to check it out.

When a man loves a woman, he thought, he's letting himself in for a lot of possible trouble along with all the pleasure his loving brings him. A jealous man like Jordan, he thought, can be turned into a murdering man when the woman who's the apple of his eye looks away from him and finds somebody else more to her liking.

He rode on and was about to turn to the right at the first cross street when he heard the anguished cry.

It had come from behind him.

And not, he believed, from any of the few widely spaced dark houses on the street. He turned the bay and galloped back the way he had come, wondering if he were on a fool's errand. Maybe the doc had come. Maybe he had hurt Eunice while he was trying to repair the damage the vigilantes had done and she had cried out in pain. Maybe it wasn't Eunice who had screamed at all. Maybe Vivian Pruitt was squeamish and it had been her who'd cried out when she saw what the doc was doing to Eunice. Fool's errand or not, he intended to find out if Eunice was all right.

When he reached the house, he leaped from the saddle and went running toward the door. Halfway to it, he halted and stepped swiftly to one side so that he could see through the window that flanked it.

His hand went to his gun as he stared through the window at the four robed and hooded vigilantes in the kitchen, one of whom was holding Eunice prisoner, her arms twisted behind her back.

One of the other vigilantes stepped forward and thrust a dirty balled-up rag into her mouth to gag her.

Armed, Cimarron thought. All four of them. I'm outgunned, he thought. He thought of his promise to protect Eunice. Then another thought crossed his mind. What if Vivian Pruitt walked in on the scene in the kitchen with the doctor? Both of them would fall into the vigilantes' hands, and those hands, he thought, will be rough ones since those men in there won't take kindly to the lady and the doc trying to help Eunice.

He looked down at the ground as he drew his .44. He ran a boot through the grass in front of him until he had uncovered a stone, which he picked up. He took up a position between the window and the door, flattening his back against the wall of the house. He threw the stone and it hit the door.

The door opened. Lamplight streamed out into the night.

"There's nobody out here," a man said from just inside the kitchen, and Cimarron recognized his voice.

"Look around outside," ordered the gruff-voiced vigilante Cimarron had heard before. "I just heard something."

When the man stepped out under the overhang, Cimarron tried to slow his heavy breathing, sure that, if he didn't, the vigilante would hear it.

He waited until the man had taken another step beyond the shallow pool of lamplight, and then he reached out with his left hand and clapped it over the man's mouth while simultaneously pulling him out from under the overhang and away from the open door. He held the struggling man tightly against him, and then, after holstering his Colt, he used his right hand to pinch the man's nostrils. The man kicked and thrashed wildly as he struggled for air, which he could not obtain because Cimarron kept his left hand clamped over his mouth and his other hand pinched on his nostrils.

As Cimarron held on, the vigilante's struggles diminished in strength and finally stopped altogether. When his captive went limp, Cimarron hauled him around to the south side of the house, dropped him, and then raced to the front door. He opened it and shouted, "Eunice!"

When he heard boots pounding toward the front door, he ran to the back of the house and looked through the window again.

He almost shouted his elation over the fact that his plan had worked—so far, at least. He threw open the back door and burst into the kitchen, his gun drawn, to confront the single vigilante who remained in the room—the one holding the still-struggling Eunice.

"Don't go for your gun," he ordered the man. "Let her go!"

The vigilante did as he had been told, and Eunice pulled the gag from her mouth and threw it on the floor. She ran to Cimarron, but before she could throw her arms around him as she obviously had been intending to do, he shoved her through the back door and quickly followed her outside.

"Take my horse," he told her. "Get out of here! Hole up somewhere!"

"But—"

"*Do it,*" he bellowed at her, and she climbed aboard the bay and went galloping off into the night.

Cimarron holstered his .44. He turned, leapt up, and caught the edge of the overhang with both hands. He hauled himself up onto it and then bellied down upon it.

Two vigilantes rounded the north side of the house. They were met by the vigilante who had been in the kitchen as he emerged from it. "He was here," the man yelped.

"Who was here?" another asked.

"That damned deputy, that's who! He got the drop on me—took the girl with him."

Someone cursed. "I just heard a horse. It must have been the two of them getting away."

"Goddamm it," a vigilante roared. "You know what you are? You're as useless as a sack of shit, that's what you are. I leave you to guard that girl and you let her get away from you. A *girl*, mind you!"

"She didn't get away from me. That goddamned deputy *took* her from me."

Cimarron heard a curse, then the sound of a fist smashing against a jaw. Then the sound of a body thudding against something. Then the sound of wood splintering.

He felt the overhang suddenly tilt beneath him, and as he suddenly fell, he realized what had happened. The man who had been damning his companion for losing Eunice had struck him and he had crashed into one of the two poles supporting the overhang and it had shattered from the impact.

Cimarron braced himself, and when he hit the ground, he swiftly scrambled to his feet . . .

To face the barrels of a sawed-off brush gun and a revolver.

And then a second revolver's barrel as the vigilante who had been struck by one of the others got to his feet and drew his gun.

One of the vigilantes snickered.

Then another.

And another.

Soon all three were laughing uproariously as Cimarron stood, not daring to draw his own gun, facing them and silently cursing their merriment that his fall had caused.

But Eunice got away, he thought. That's some consolation.

"Kill the bastard—right now!" one of the vigilantes muttered as their laughter weakened and died. "We've tried to before and he always gets away from us. Kill him!"

Cimarron heard the click of a gun's hammer being drawn back. He stared down at the cocked revolver in the steady hand of the vigilante who was standing next to the one with the brush gun.

Vivian Pruitt suddenly appeared in the open kitchen door,

and when she saw Cimarron and the vigilantes gathered just beyond the broken overhang, she took a step backward.

Cimarron, as the vigilantes turned toward her, suddenly lashed out with a stiff right arm and knocked the cocked gun from the hand of the man who had been about to shoot him. At the same time, he yelled to Vivian, "Get out of here! Into the house!"

He dropped to his knees as one of the other vigilantes fired at him and the bullet whined harmlessly over his head. He lunged forward, seized the man behind the knees, and pulled him off his feet. As the man went down and dropped his gun, Cimarron drew his Colt and fired at the vigilante closest to him.

His bullet caught the man in the shoulder, spinning him around.

"Into the house!" he shouted to Vivian a second time, and this time she obeyed him. As she turned and fled into the house, he fired again and the gun flew from the hand of one of the other vigilantes.

A wild whoop suddenly split the night. It was followed by a shouted command: "Don't nobody move. Drop your guns!"

The vigilantes—including the one Cimarron had rendered unconscious earlier when he had cut off the man's air supply and who had just wandered groggily around the side of the house—stiffened into immobility, dropped their guns, and looked up at the window above the broken overhang from which a rifle barrel protruded.

Cimarron got slowly to his feet as men rounded both sides of the house, all of them armed. As they moved closer, he recognized Cloud, Black Dirt, Mad Wolf, and Wild Cat among them. He looked up at the window, squinting at the man whose face was hidden in the darkness.

"Cimarron, what the hell would you do if I weren't around to look out for you?" The question had been asked by the man in the window, and Cimarron recognized Jimmy Jumper's voice.

"I was doing well enough, Jumper. Shot me one jasper already. Would have shot me a few more."

"Maybe they would have shot you. Did you ever think of that?"

"I did. What the hell are you doing here, Jumper?"

Jumper climbed out the window and slid down the overhang which slanted down to the ground as it leaned crazily from its one remaining upright. "Wild Cat trailed one of the vigilantes that got away from us before, and then he doubled back and found the rest of us Red Sticks. We were out beating the bushes looking for them. When he found us, we followed him into town and he showed us where the one he had trailed had holed up. But before we could get our hands on him, he hightailed it here. We decided maybe that one would lead us to the rest of them, and so he did. I came into the house—the front door was open—and went upstairs to that window up there.

"The rest of us Red Sticks took up positions on both sides of the house. We'd agreed there'd be no shooting if we could get the drop on them. We didn't want to shoot you, Deputy, and you were, for a while there, right in the middle of this bad bunch. But then you started that ruckus just now and I figured it was time for the rest of us to join in."

"Help me keep them covered," Cimarron said, and walked toward the man he had shot in the shoulder.

"Help *you* keep them covered?" Jumper roared. "That's a hot one, that is. It's more like you're helping us keep them covered."

"Have it your way, Jumper," Cimarron said offhandedly as he pulled the hood from the head of the wounded man.

"That's the one Wild Cat followed," Jumper said. "To the livery stable," he added.

Cimarron stared at Buster Schuyler, who avoided his eyes. "Tell me something, Schuyler," he said. "You didn't spy on the vigilantes who were crucifying Cassidy, did you?" Without waiting for an answer, he continued, "You *helped* them crucify Cassidy." When Schuyler said nothing, Cimarron reached out and slammed a fist against Schuyler's wounded shoulder.

163

Schuyler screamed.

"Answer me, goddammit!" Cimarron muttered.

"Yes," Schuyler bellowed. "I did!"

"Thought so. When you were telling me what you claimed you only saw—Schuyler, you sounded to me the way most men sound when they're talking about a woman they'd like to lay. You sounded *hot*, Schuyler. Like you were getting ready to *come!*"

Cimarron suddenly turned to the left and ripped the hood from a second vigilante.

"He's a sadist, Schuyler is!" the unmasked August Child screeched. "That's the only reason he joined us. Unlike the rest of us, Schuyler enjoys doing what we have to do."

"Have to do, Child?" Cimarron prodded.

"Yes," Child replied defiantly. He pointed to Jumper, who was staring at him through narrowed eyes. "We felt it was our civic duty to attempt to wreak vengeance on that rapist and murderer!"

"Jumper didn't rape, nor did he murder, Clementine Jordan."

"He—"

"Shut up, Child! You wanted to hunt him down so's he wouldn't be able to blow the whistle on you for stealing from the tribal treasury. You didn't give so much as a shit whether or not he was guilty of the crimes committed against Clementine Jordan."

"That's not true," Child protested. "Jumper's charges against me are false and baseless."

"Maybe so and maybe not. The fact remains you stand accused, and it's a matter for your Seminole tribal council to settle, so I plan on turning you over to the Lighthorsemen." Cimarron reached for the hood of a third vigilante, but before he could touch it, the man himself pulled it off and, smiling, said, " 'Evening, Mr. Deputy."

" 'Evening, Possum Jack," Cimarron said, suppressing his surprise. "I didn't expect to find you hiding under one of those hoods."

"Well, it does look like you've gone and found me, don't

it? To tell you the total truth, I thought it might all wind up this way, seeing as how you be such a *persistent* man, Mister Deputy."

"You mind telling me what turned you into a vigilante?"

"Might as well as not," Possum Jack Tucker said amiably. But then, his eyes blazing and his finger pointing directly at Jimmy Jumper, he snarled, "*Him!* It was him and his daddy and his daddy before him and what all them mens did to me and my daddy and his daddy afore him."

Cimarron, remembering what Possum Jack had told him about the pre-Civil War days at the Seminole festival, said. "You're talking about the Jumper family's slave-holding days, I take it."

"Us black folks never had enough food to put in our bellies, nor enough clothes to put upon our backs. Those Jumpers was mean mens, Mister Deputy, and I bear the marks of their whips on my body to prove. I ain't just imagining wrongs that wasn't never done to me—to me and mine. Even to the oldest two of my chilluns, who catched rickets on account of what they didn't have to eat most days."

"So you joined up with this bunch to get even with—"

"The Jumper clan," Possum Jack interrupted.

"You're a lying son of a bitch," Jumper shouted, shaking a fist at Possum Jack. "We took good care of all our slaves!"

"I ain't telling nothing but the truth, Massa Jimmy! You Jumpers slopped your hogs far better than you ever did us."

Massa Jimmy, Cimarron thought. The old ways and days, they do die hard in a hurt and hating man's mind. He ripped the hood from the fourth vigilante to find himself confronting a cringing Clay Jordan.

"I was surprised," Cimarron said, "when I found out that old Possum Jack there was vigilante. I was about as much surprised to find that August Child was riding with you boys. But, Jordan, I'm not a bit surprised to find out you're a vigilante, too. Fact is, I recognized your voice when you came out of the house after I threw that stone at the door to draw one or more of you outside."

"Don't you dare lay a hand on me again," Jordan cried, backing abruptly away from Cimarron. "You was almost the death of me, cutting off my air the way you went and did before when I came out of the house."

"Jordan, I'm arresting you for the rape and murder of your wife, and I'm taking you along with the rest of your vigilante friends back to Fort Smith to stand trial for rape, murder, assault, battery—"

"Jordan!" Vivian snarled as she suddenly emerged again from the house. "Is what this deputy just said true?"

"No," Jordan bellowed, "he's lying. Ask my daughter. She saw what happened. She saw that no-good Injun—"

"Miss Pruitt," Cimarron said, interrupting Jordan, "it's true what I said. Eunice told me she'd been lying all along about what happened on account of her daddy here promised to kill her, too, if she told the truth about what she saw him do to her ma.

"Seems Mrs. Jordan had Elmer Bennett take some nude photographs of her. They were to be a present for a lover she'd taken on. Jordan saw them and he killed his wife on account of them."

Vivian, moving with the swiftness of an antelope, darted past Cimarron, stooped, and picked up one of the revolvers that had been dropped by one of the vigilantes. Holding it in both hands and aiming it at Jordan, she screeched, "Those pictures were for *me,* Jordan! Clementine was going to leave you and she and I were going to go away together. She had had quite enough of your bestiality and of your brutality to her in bed and out of it. When we became lovers, she told me she'd never in her life known that loving another human being could be so wonderful. So full of grace and gentility, she said."

The Red Sticks began to mumble to one another in low tones as they darted disgusted glances in Vivian's direction.

"I'm going to kill you, Clay Jordan," she declared coldly. "You're not fit to live. It's men like you who defile the very name of love and turn the world itself into a vile place."

Cimarron grabbed for the gun in Vivian's hand, but she wheeled away from him and fired.

"Jee-*sus!*" Jordan bellowed as he clutched his left thigh where the bullet had struck him. "You goddamned *bitch,* you!"

Cimarron tore the gun from Vivian's hand before she could fire a second time.

"You oughtn't to have done that to Mister Jordan, Miss Pruitt," Possum Jack said dolefully.

"Possum Jack's right," Schuyler exclaimed, still holding his wounded shoulder. "He was one of us the same as you are yourself."

"Well, now," Cimarron said, his voice close to a sigh, "so that's how the vigilantes knew where Eunice and me were."

Vivian turned away from him as he continued, "You weren't going for any damned doctor, were you, Miss Pruitt? You hightailed it out of your house to go round up your vigilante friends to come kill me and maybe Eunice too."

Vivian whirled to face Cimarron and, her eyes on fire, shouted, "To kill *you!* Not Eunice. Eunice—we would have punished her, but not killed her." She suddenly crumpled to the ground.

"What's the matter with her?" Jordan barked.

"Fainted," Cimarron said, and then instantly realized how wrong he had been about what he had thought had happened to Vivian as she swiftly rose to her knees, another of the vigilante's dropped guns clutched tightly in her hands.

She cocked it, aiming at Cimarron, a demented smile twisting her features.

"Drop it," shouted someone Cimarron couldn't see from behind the group of Red Sticks, but Vivian fired. Just before she did so, Cimarron had thrown himself flat on the ground and the bullet went over him and struck Wild Cat. He clutched his chest, made a wet gurgling sound, and collapsed lifeless on the ground.

The Seminole Lighthorseman who had ordered Vivian to drop the gun shouldered his way through the Red Sticks, his gun drawn. As Vivian swiveled around, ready to fire at him, he fired first: and Vivian, struck just below her waist, dropped the gun in her hand and fell to the ground.

"Finish off the rest of those vigilante bastards," Jumper yelled and fired, hitting and killing Clay Jordan.

Cimarron aimed the gun he had taken from Vivian earlier and his own .44 at Jumper as two more Lighthorsemen appeared from around the south side of the house. "No more killing, Jumper," he said.

Jumper wavered, the gun in his hand slowly swinging around to point at Cimarron.

The other Red Sticks remained motionless as they watched their leader.

"You fast, Jumper?" Cimarron asked. "Want to bet I'm faster?"

One of the Lighthorsemen stepped forward and quickly disarmed Jumper. The other two Lighthorsemen did the same for the other Red Sticks. One of them took the gun Cimarron handed to him—one of the two Vivian had retrieved from the ground earlier—and then scooped up the guns that remained on the ground.

"I'm sure glad to see you, boys," Cimarron told the Lighthorsemen as he holstered his .44. "You joined the party at just the right time. How come you did? You heard the noise we were making?"

The Lighthorseman who had disarmed Jumper shook his head and then called over his shoulder. "Miss Jordan, it's safe for you to come out now."

Eunice came into sight moments later from around the corner of the house. She hesitated, looked down at her father and Vivian, and then she ran to Cimarron, threw her arms around him, and asked, "Are you all right?"

"I'm fine, honey."

"I couldn't just ride off and leave you to face those men all alone. I went straight to the house where I knew a Lighthorseman lived and I told him what was going on here. He rounded up some of his men and— Oh, I'm so glad you're not hurt." She looked up at Cimarron. "My pa—he's dead?"

168

Cimarron nodded.

"Was it you who killed him?"

"Nope. Jumper did."

"Why?"

"Him and his Red Sticks were out to get revenge on the vigilantes in the name of his people."

"Miss Pruitt?"

"She was aiming to kill me. That Lighthorseman over there got her before she could." Cimarron turned to the man who seemed to be the leader of the Lighthorsemen, the one who had first appeared on the scene. "You'll clear these corpses out of here, will you?"

When the Lighthorseman nodded, Cimarron continued, "I'd be much obliged to you if you'd take these vigilantes into custody. August Child there, he's been stealing from your tribal treasury, according to Jumper, so he's yours to deal with. Hold Schuyler and Possum Jack for me to pick up later. Hold Jumper for me, too."

"On what charge?" Jumper bellowed at Cimarron.

"Murder. You killed Clay Jordan and those two white boys a while back. I reckon your daddy's going to be mighty disappointed when he hears you'll hang for your hotheadedness."

Jumper angrily shook his head in denial of Cimarron's charges "*Cap-pe-tum-nee-lox-au!*" he spat.

"Now, I can tell you there's no use in you denying what you did, and I want to ask you what the hell it is you're saying to me."

The leader of the Seminole Lighthorsemen spoke. "He just called you prince of liars, Deputy."

"Oh, he did, did he?" Cimarron turned to the Red Sticks gathered around Jumper. "Black Dirt, you and Mad Wolf and Cloud and the rest of you are free to go. You are, that is, if you're willing to testify in court later on that I'm no prince of liars, on account of you all saw Jumper kill Clay Jordan and those two boys, same as me. But if it turns out you're not willing to testify, well, then, I'll have to take you all back to Arkansas with me right along with Jumper and Schuyler and

Possum Jack. As accomplices to those two murders I just mentioned.''

The Red Sticks glanced at one another, whispered together briefly, and then Mad Wolf said, "We will testify."

"Good," Cimarron said. "Glad to get your cooperation." He stood and watched as the Lighthorsemen herded Jumper, Child, Schuyler, and Possum Jack away. When they had all disappeared, he put an arm around Eunice and said softly, "I'm real sorry about what happened to your pa, honey."

"I shouldn't say it—it's a terrible thing to say, a truly awful thing—but I'm not sorry. The fact is, I can't feel anything for him. I don't even want to see to his burying.'' Her eyes lingered briefly on Jordan's corpse and then drifted away. "If you'd been there that night he killed Ma, you wouldn't be sorry neither.'' Eunice paused a moment and then added, "There's something I don't altogether understand.''

"What's that?"

"Miss Pruitt. You said she was trying to kill you. Now, why would she want to do a thing like that?"

"It turns out she rode with the vigilantes and had as good a reason as any of the rest of them for wanting me out of the way.''

"I wonder how Ma could have been good friends with a woman like that."

"It's time you were heading home, honey," Cimarron said, hoping to ward off any further speculations or questions from Eunice about her mother and Vivian Pruitt.

"Yes, I guess it is." She hesitated a moment and then said, "I want to thank you for all you've done for me, Cimarron.''

"No thanks needed, honey."

"Considering all you've done for me, it seems shameful of me to ask you to do one more thing."

"You ask it. I'll do it. Be glad to."

"Would you do me the favor of seeing me home? I could walk but—''

"Honey, I'd all along had every intention of seeing you home. That's not doing you any favor. That's pleasuring myself."

Eunice gave him a faint smile and then took his hand and led him around the house to where she had left his bay.

1

As Cimarron rode his bay through the torrents of rain, a flash of
forked lightning illuminated the midmorning sky.

He bent his head until his chin was almost touching his chest
to allow the heavy rain to pour freely from the brim of his black
flat-topped stetson. As he did so, thunder cannonaded through
the San Bois Mountains surrounding him. He felt the bay beneath him flinch at the ominous sound but gamely continue to
pick its way through the thick cross timbers whose branches
touched the ground as they bent low because of the rain's wet
weight on their leaves.

As the echoes of the thunder gradually faded, the sky was
again sundered by lightning. Then, again, only a brief moment
later, more thunder boomed and moaned as its sound first
richocheted off the mountains' peaks and then went rolling
down into the valleys.

The creaking of Cimarron's saddle was drowned by the
thunder as was the crackling of the yellow oilskin slicker he

was wearing, which he had spread out over his horse's rump to keep his bedroll dry.

If this horse under me had fins and some gills, he thought wryly, we'd make a whole lot faster progress. He rode on doggedly, the water pouring from his hat to splash on the bay's mane and neck and add to the flood that was already streaming down the animal's body.

But ten minutes later, the summer storm had moved southward toward the Winding Stair Mountains, its thunder merely mutterings now in the distance. Gradually, the rain slowed and then it finally stopped. Breaks began to appear in the dark clouds. A shaft of sunlight speared through one of them and the raindrops that were clinging to the leaves of the trees began to glisten with bright colors, becoming rubies, emeralds, and garnets before they fattened and fell into oblivion on the boggy ground below.

Cimarron, when he reached the Poteau River, rode along its winding western bank in a southerly direction. When he came to Jake Ransom's cabin, which was not far from the river's bank, he hallooed it, his wet hands clasped around his saddle horn, his green eyes on its closed door.

He hallooed it again, and this time his call brought results. A grizzled, middle-aged man opened the door, a shotgun in his hands. He peered up at Cimarron and then frowned.

"Howdy, Jake. Some storm, huh?"

"What you want, Deputy?"

"Now, Jake, is that any way to greet a man who's just come through what was far worse than what old Noah ever had to put up with? A man who'd dismount if he were asked to and who'd welcome a hot cup of coffee were he to be offered one?"

"I ain't asking you to dismount, Deputy, nor am I running a soup kitchen here."

Cimarron's eyes hardened as he stared steadily at Jake. "The last time I was passing through these parts, Jake, you almost shot me with that scatter gun of yours. It seems you've mellowed some—though not much—since then."

Jake raised the barrel of his shotgun.

"Have it your way, then. I'll be moseying on. But before I go, I want to let you know that I've been trailing a man name of Ray Biddle. He gave me the slip about five miles south of Poteau when the rain started and washed away his tracks. I've

174

been following what amounts to a blind trail since then. You happen to have seen any strangers come by here lately, Jake?"

"What I see or don't see is my business, not the law's."

"I'd sort of hoped you'd be in more of a frame of mind to lend me a hand this time out, Jake."

"Well, I'm not, and you know damned well why I'm not. I'm not for the same reason I wouldn't talk to you the other times you came by here prying. I'm not because Indian Territory's infested with hardcases, and a man who wants to keep himself all in one piece, well, it pays him to keep his eyes and ears open and his mouth shut if he don't want some big-gunned bastard taking him for a target because he went and told tales to the law."

"I can see your point, Jake, though I surely do regret the stand you're taking."

As Cimarron was about to turn his bay, ready to ride away from the cabin, Jake asked, "What's this Biddle fella done that's got you out after his ass?"

"He's an amorous man, Biddle is. Seems one woman's not enough for him. Biddle's a bigamist. He went and married three women in the last year. Three that we know of, that is."

"That sort of puts him to row in the same boat as you, don't it, Deputy?" Jake cackled. "From what I've heard told about you, one woman, or even a hundred's not near enough for you."

"But there's a difference between Biddle and me, Jake," Cimarron responded cheerfully. "I don't marry my women, so I manage to stay on the safe side of the law."

"You'd best watch where you step, Deputy. Biddle just might try to take a potshot or two at you."

"He might, but I'm a fairly tough-hided hombre. I reckon that's on account of where I come from. Texas is a real tough country. Why, Jake, that country where I was foaled is so damned tough that down there the hoot owls, they all sing bass."

Cimarron rode away from the cabin, still heading south along the river, until he came to a small clearing at the base of one of the San Bois' slopes. There he dismounted, removed his slicker, folded it, and tied it behind the cantle of his saddle next to his bedroll. He took some jerky from one of his saddlebags, and leaning back against the trunk of a piñon pine, he began to chew it as his eyes roamed the surrounding countryside.

The mountain slope opposite him on the far side of the gorge through which the Poteau River wound was covered with piñon pines and shin oaks. The wet needles and leaves of the trees seemed to gleam a brighter green in the slanting sunlight. To the north, the gorge and the river angled westward and out of sight. To the south, the river stretched in an almost straight line, sunlight glinting on its smooth surface, and the gorge deepened in that direction because of the increased height of the slopes rising on either side of it.

Cimarron listened to the racket unseen birds were making. He felt the warm sun on his shoulders as he chewed the tough meat. He heard the faint murmur of the river and the whispers of the light wind as it roved through the cross timbers, scattering remaining raindrops through the clear and sweet-smelling air.

Maybe I've gone and lost Biddle, he thought. He could have turned east toward Arkansas or headed west deeper into the Territory while I kept on traveling south after him. But he's been heading south ever since I picked up his trail just south of Poteau. He could be hiding up there right now, in any one of those nooks and crannies of that slope, he thought, his eyes scanning its thickly forested landscape. With a rifle, he thought.

He didn't know if Biddle was armed, but he did know that the man was a fool if he wasn't. The bar dog he'd questioned in Poteau had told him that Biddle had been in the saloon and that he'd bought beer. He also could have bought a gun while he was in town, Cimarron thought, figuring rightly that the law'd be sure to be out after him, since one of his wives had told him she'd gone to Marshal Upham in Fort Smith to tell him her tale of woe when she'd found out that her dearly beloved Biddle had married two other willing ladies besides herself.

Cimarron swallowed the last of his jerky and made up his mind to continue his southward journey, promising himself that, if he found no plain trail once the ground had dried, he'd double back and start asking questions of everyone who lived in the vicinity.

He swung into the saddle and was about to move out when a flash of light halted him. He turned and looked back the way he had come. Had he really seen a flash of light? Or had he merely imagined it? If he hadn't imagined it, could it have been the sun striking mica somewhere up on the slope behind him?

As he gazed northward, the bright flash came again and this time he saw its source—high up on the western slope. He watched the spot intently and was rewarded by a third flash. Mirror, he thought. Somebody's signaling somebody. He turned an instant after the fourth flash glittered from the slope. Whoever's using that mirror's aiming it right over that way—at the mountaintop across the river, he realized.

An answering flash appeared from the peak Cimarron was staring at so intently, and he heeled his bay. He found a shallow spot and forded the river. Then, when he reached the base of the slope, he dug his boot heels into his bay's ribs to urge it onward and then upward.

Whoever's signaling back and forth, he thought as the hooves of the animal under him occasionally slipped on the steep terrain, well, it could all be as harmless a pastime as dancing the polka. But maybe it's not. Maybe somebody's sending some kind of message to somebody that I ought to know about.

The bay angled upward slowly, blowing and fighting the bit in its mouth, until it reached a level but narrow ridge.

Cimarron drew rein and slid out of the saddle. After tethering his horse to a tree and pulling his '73 Winchester from its saddle scabbard, he started to climb what remained of the slope on foot, weaving in and out between the thick trees, using them at times as handholds to pull himself upward. When he neared the mountain's summit, he slowed his pace and then halted to crouch down behind a piñon. From his vantage point, he peered upward but saw no more signals. He turned and looked down the slope in both directions. Almost at once, he spotted the cabin, not far below him on the left. One of its walls sagged and its roof tilted downward on that side. Its door lay broken on the ground in front of the cabin, almost completely hidden by tall weeds and some sprouting seedlings of shin oaks.

He heard the snap of twigs and the rustle of underbrush. He dropped down to lie flat on the ground, his rifle in both hands, its barrel aimed at the spot from which the sounds had come as someone or something moved hurriedly through the forest.

He grinned when Ray Biddle, slipping and sliding as he scurried down from the mountain's summit toward the obviously abandoned cabin below, came into sight.

Cimarron rose to one knee, aimed, fired.

The bullet struck the ground a few feet in front of Biddle, causing him to cry out wordlessly and halt.

Cimarron stood up and yelled, "Hold it right there, Biddle."

As his quarry turned alarmed eyes on him, Cimarron made his way toward the man, ignoring the low-hanging branches that switched his face, his rifle held in both hands and aimed directly at Biddle's chest. When he was within a few yards of Biddle, he halted. "Get your horse," he ordered.

Biddle shook his head.

"You do as you're told, Biddle, else I'll have to teach you how to be obedient, and let me tell you straight and true that I can be a real mean taskmaster."

"It's dead," Biddle said tonelessly. "It fell and broke its leg. I had to shoot it."

So Biddle's got some kind of gun, Cimarron thought, although he saw none. Somewhere he's got one. Maybe in that abandoned cabin where I reckon he's been holed up. "Start walking down the slope, Biddle," he commanded. "Keep your hands high. I'll be right behind you."

Biddle obeyed.

The two men walked without speaking for several minutes before Biddle broke the silence.

"What I did didn't hurt anybody, Cimarron. What I did, it made some women pretty happy."

"You know me, do you?"

"Somebody in Fort Smith once pointed you out to me." Biddle halted. "From what they told me about you, I figure you ought to be able to understand about me and those women I met and married. By all accounts, you're more of a stud than I could ever hope to be."

"I don't know if that's a compliment you're paying me or not, Biddle, and I don't much care. *Move!*"

"I've got money," Biddle said slyly, not moving. "The last lady I married was rich."

"I've got a rifle, Biddle, and if I use it on you, the money you speak of won't do you a damned bit of good. Now, get your ass on down the mountain."

Cimarron strode up to Biddle and buried the muzzle of his rifle in the small of the man's back.

Biddle shrugged and took a step forward. Suddenly, he spun around, his stiff right arm a flail. It struck the barrel of Cimarron's rifle, knocking it to the left, and before Cimarron could swing it back into position, Biddle seized it and yanked it from his hands.

Holding it by the barrel in both hands and using it as a club, he swung on Cimarron, who ducked down low so that the rifle butt went harmlessly over his head. He lunged forward and tackled Biddle around the knees, toppling the man.

Biddle gave a grunt, sat up swiftly, and slammed the rifle butt against the back of Cimarron's head, knocking Cimarron's hat off.

Cimarron released his hold on Biddle's legs and drove a hard right fist into the man's groin. Biddle screamed in agony and dropped the rifle. Cimarron swiftly retrieved it, sprang to his feet, and stood breathing fast and staring down at Biddle, who lay curled up on the ground, both hands frantically clutching his groin.

"Get up, Biddle!"

"Can't."

Cimarron reached down with his left hand. He seized Biddle's shirt collar and hauled the man, who was groaning piteously, to his feet. Then, still holding on to him with one hand and prodding him with his rifle barrel, he marched him down through the trees toward the ridge where he had left his bay.

When he reached the ridge, he released Biddle and rummaged about in his saddlebags until he found his handcuffs. He handed them to Biddle, who reluctantly took them from him and looked down at them as if they were some kind of loathsome insects for which he felt nothing but disgust.

"Put them on, Biddle."

Biddle, his body bent forward as he favored his injured groin, snapped one cuff around his left wrist. He started to snap the remaining one around his right wrist, but then, giving a wild cry, he doubled over and began to howl, his hands once again clutching his groin as if it had been only a moment ago that Cimarron had savaged him there.

Cimarron, ignoring the man's cries of pain, reached out to

fasten the remaining cuff, and as he did so, Biddle suddenly straightened, silent now, his face a mask of cold hatred. He swung the free cuff that dangled from its chain and the metal slashed the right side of Cimarron's face.

Cimarron sprang forward, reaching out with his free hand to grab Biddle. But Biddle quickly stepped backward and to one side, and as Cimarron lunged past him, he lifted his right leg and viciously kicked Cimarron in the buttocks, knocking him to his knees. Before Cimarron could recover from the attack, Biddle kicked him again and he went over the edge of the ridge. As he started to slide down the slope after his rifle, which eventually disappeared in the underbrush, he managed to grab a flat rock that protruded at an angle from the lip of the ridge. He brought up his free hand and gripped the rock, and with his boots dislodging dirt and loose shale, he tried to fight his way back onto the ridge.

Biddle's boot heel smashed down on his left hand.

Cimarron clenched his teeth against the pain and continued to struggle upward.

Biddle's right boot heel smashed down on his right hand and then on his left hand a second time.

Cimarron's left hand reflexively let go of the rock. Biddle raised his boot to stomp Cimarron's right hand, which still clutched the rock with whitened fingers, but Cimarron reached up with his pain-ridden left hand and seized Biddle by the ankle. At the same time, he let go of the rock and Biddle pitched forward. Both men went rolling down the slope, their bodies bouncing off each other, until Cimarron struck a tree that stopped his slide.

Almost instantly he was on his feet. He went racing down the slope after the still-tumbling Biddle. When he caught up with the man, he hauled him to his feet, got both of his hands around Biddle's thick neck, and began to squeeze, simultaneously slamming the back of Biddle's head against the stout trunk of a loblolly pine.

Within seconds, Biddle's body went limp and Cimarron let him go. As the unconscious Biddle slumped to the ground at his feet, Cimarron reached down and snapped the loose handcuff around his prisoner's right wrist.

Then he turned and climbed up beyond the ridge to the spot where he had lost his hat. When he had retrieved it, he made his way back down the slope past the ridge and past Biddle. It took him several minutes of careful searching before he finally found his Winchester lodged in a thick tangle of underbrush. He made his way back up the slope to where Biddle lay. He dragged the unconscious man up to the ridge. There he booted his rifle, removed the rope that hung from his saddle horn, and tied, using a solid square knot, one end of it to the chain that linked Biddle's handcuffs.

By the time he was finished, Biddle had regained consciousness.

"Who signaled you?" Cimarron asked.

Biddle, staring down at Cimarron's handiwork, muttered, "Damn your stinking soul, Deputy!"

Cimarron patiently repeated his question, and when Biddle didn't answer it, he punctuated it with a kick to Biddle's ribs.

"Jake Ransom," Biddle said, raising his hands to shield his body as Cimarron's right foot swung backward, prepared to kick him a second time.

"Why?"

"I paid him—paid him good—to warn me if there were any lawmen in the area. I kept watch up on the mountain above the abandoned cabin I was using."

"And he signaled you that I was around and about, and you signaled him back that you'd got his message. Didn't do you much good, though, did it?" Without waiting for an answer, Cimarron swung into the saddle, and after taking a few dallies around the saddle horn with his rope, he started the bay down the slope at a slow walk, forcing the bound Biddle to follow him on foot.

When he reached Jake Ransom's cabin, he dismounted and threw open the unlocked door to find the one-room building empty. His eyes scanned the dim interior of the cabin, and then, when he spotted Jake's shotgun resting on two pegs on one of the walls, he slammed the door and leaned back against it, prepared to wait.

Only minutes later, Jake rounded the cabin and stopped short when he saw his visitors.

"Howdy, Jake," Cimarron said pleasantly but with no trace of a smile. "We've been waiting for you."

"Why've you been waiting for me?"

Cimarron unleathered his Colt and aimed it almost nonchalantly at the unarmed Jake, who began to splutter a garbled protest.

"You're coming with Biddle and me, Jake."

"What for?"

"For aiding and abetting."

"What're you talking about?" Jake thundered angrily.

"You aided a fugitive from the law. You abetted him in his attempt to escape from the law. Both of those things are crimes."

"I didn't!" Jake roared as Cimarron freed his rope from his saddle horn and took a second pair of handcuffs from one of his saddlebags. After holstering his Colt and then snapping the cuffs on Jake's wrists, he looped the rope twice around the chain linking the cuffs before climbing back into the saddle. Then he twisted the rope around his saddle horn and moved out.

"You told him," Jake shouted from behind Cimarron.

"I had to," Biddle bellowed. "He would have killed me if I hadn't!"

Cimarron glanced over his shoulder and grinned as he saw Jake give Biddle a furious kick and Biddle retaliate by giving Jake a hard jab in the ribs with his elbow.

Cimarron turned around and rode on, heading northeast toward Fort Smith as Biddle and Jake, trotting along behind the bay, continued to bicker loudly.

Two days later, in the early morning, Cimarron rode through the gate into the Fort Smith courtyard, where the gallows and courthouse stood inside a low stone wall.

He headed for the courthouse beyond the gallows and drew rein in front of the ground-level door that led to the jail in the basement of the courthouse. He threw his left leg over his saddle horn and slid down off his horse. Without even glancing at his two prisoners, who were silently sullen now, he pounded on the door. It was opened almost immediately by Charley Burns, the jailer.

"Good day to you, Cimarron," Burns greeted him. "What have you got for me this time?"

Cimarron pointed. "That's Biddle, the bigamist I was out after. The other jasper's Jake Ransom, who used to make his home down in the San Bois Mountains but is about to take up lodgings in your establishment, Charley, on account of he was trying to help Biddle dodge the law."

"It's pretty crowded inside," Charley commented, "but I guess I can squeeze these two fellows in."

Cimarron removed his rope from his saddle horn and then from the handcuff chains as Charley held his six-gun on Biddle and Jake. He thrust a hand into the pocket of his jeans and pulled out a key, which he used to unlock the handcuffs. "They're all yours now, Charley."

Burns gestured with his gun and Biddle and Jake went meekly through the door and into the corridor. At the other end, another door opened onto the jail itself.

Cimarron was replacing the two pair of handcuffs in his saddlebag when Charley returned and said, "I've been told that Marshal Upham wants to see me, but my assistant jailer hasn't shown up this morning. I'm wondering, Cimarron, if you'd take over here for a spell—just long enough for me to go see what Upham wants with me."

"Be glad to, Charley."

"That lime there," Charley said, pointing to a bucket on the ground next to the locked door, "wants sprinkling on the floor inside the jail. That place stinks worse than a pair of sties set side by side. I'm wondering, would you mind?"

"I'll sprinkle it, Charley. You go on about your business."

When Burns had given him his jail key and gone, Cimarron stood for a moment watching the men and women entering and leaving the courthouse. His eyes eagerly and longingly trailed a buxom woman in a yellow silk dress and blue bonnet as she climbed the steps of the courthouse, her long skirt held up by one delicate hand.

He grinned as a man who was not far behind the woman stumbled on the steps because his eyes, like Cimarron's, had been on the woman's trim ankles.

He turned to find two mounted men, one of them leading a saddled and bridled but riderless mount, approaching him.

"Pretty, wasn't she?" the man riding ahead of his companion, who was leading the third horse, commented.

Cimarron nodded, noting that the paleness of the man's face was emphasized by the starkly contrasting blackness of his long hair and thick mustache. His gray eyes were expressionless as he stared past Cimarron at the courthouse. He was almost as tall as Cimarron and he wore two revolvers strapped around his waist beneath his canvas duster.

"Court must be in session," he speculated as he dismounted. "Lots of people coming and going this morning."

Cimarron said nothing, his eyes on the man's companion, who was blunt-featured and whose eyebrows formed one thick line above his hard brown eyes. The man's lips turned downward at the corners.

"Do you, like me and my partner here, have business with the court?" the mustachioed man asked pleasantly.

"You might say that, seeing as how I'm one of the court's deputies, though at the moment I'm filling in as jailer for a friend of mine."

Cimarron bent down, intending to pick up the bucket of lime, but before he could do so, the man who had just dismounted, said, "I wonder if you could tell me how to find Judge Parker's chambers, Deputy."

Cimarron straightened. "You go in the front door of the courthouse over there—"

The man stepped around Cimarron, and the deputy moved up to stand beside him. "You go up to the second floor—there's a staircase just inside the front door—and then you turn right and go down the hall to where you'll find a door with the judge's name on it—on a little brass plate nailed to the door. That's his window right up there."

Cimarron became aware that the man to whom he was giving directions no longer stood beside him. He turned to find him standing several paces behind him, his duster buttoned and his hands thrust into its pockets.

"I think I've got it," the man said. "Up the steps, turn right, go down the hall—yes, I'm certain I have it. I do thank you kindly for directing me, Deputy."

Cimarron watched the man walk away, leading his horse and followed by his mounted companion. Then he bent down, picked up the bucket of lime, and unlocked the jail door with the key Burns had given him. He stepped through it, locked it behind him, and made his way down the hall to the door at its far end. After unlocking the second door, he stepped into the enormous room that served as the Fort Smith jail. His lips twisted in an involuntary grimace as the overpowering stench of human urine and feces invaded his nostrils from the buckets that had been placed in the stone chimneys to serve as latrines.

He locked the door behind him, and conscious of Ray Biddle

and Jake Ransom glaring at him from opposite sides of the filthy room, he scooped up a handful of lime and sprinkled it on the floor. A thin white mist drifted up from the floor as the men in the jail watched him, some uneasily, some with scowls on their faces.

One of the prisoners—a stockily built man with huge shoulders and hands like hams—hurried up to Cimarron, and as he did so, Cimarron's right hand, whitened by lime, went to the butt of his gun.

"No need to be nervous," the prisoner assured him hastily. "I'm a trusty. Name's Sturgis, Cy Sturgis. If you're not all that fond of what you're doing, I'll be glad to do it for you."

Cimarron wordlessly handed Sturgis the bucket and turned to unlock the door. He sneezed and then coughed as a thick cloud of lime dust suddenly rose around him. He turned to find that Sturgis had dumped the entire contents of the bucket on the floor and was now standing facing him, a lime-whitened Remington Frontier .45 held tightly in both hands.

The gun was aimed directly at Cimarron, who raised his hands above his head.

Sturgis' lips parted in a triumphant smile. "I'm obliged to you for bringing this gun to me."

Cimarron silently damned himself for a fool and worse: he had, he realized, unwittingly smuggled the gun Sturgis was now aiming at him into the jail hidden in the bucket of lime.

Sturgis' smile broadened and brightened as he watched Cimarron's expression turn sour. "Jimmy," he yelled as the other prisoners stood warily watching the proceedings. "Let's get out of this hellhole, Jimmy!"

Cimarron saw a brawny man elbow his way through the throng of prisoners and head toward Sturgis, his dark face solemn, his dark-brown eyes glittering on either side of the flat bridge above his hooked nose. Half-blood, he thought.

"Open the door!" Sturgis commanded, and Cimarron turned to obey the order.

As he swung the door open, several prisoners made a dash for it. He turned just in time to see the prisoner Jimmy pull out a spoon that had been honed to a sharp deadly point and plunge it into the nearest prisoner's gut.

The prisoners quickly dropped back as their companion fell to his knees clutching his stomach and gagging.

"Anybody else gets in our way," Sturgis announced, "and

Jimmy here will gut him, too. That understood, gents? Now, let's go, Jimmy."

Cimarron, his hands still held high above his head, walked down the corridor, Sturgis and Jimmy walking directly behind him. When he felt the muzzle of Sturgis' Remington bite into his back, he unlocked the jail's outer door and then opened it.

He halted just outside the door and stared up at the two riders flanking it. One was the man he had spoken to before entering the jail and the other was the man's silent companion. Then his eyes shifted to the wide-eyed woman—the one he had watched enter the courthouse earlier—who sat astride the third horse just behind its saddle, a gag in her mouth and her hands bound behind her back.

"Jimmy, you get up in front of the lady," Sturgis ordered, and then he climbed up behind the man with the black mustache whose bland gray eyes were on Cimarron and who held a six-gun aimed at him.

"You buried one of your guns in that bucket of lime," Cimarron stated, his eyes on the man's lime-flecked gun hand.

"We have taken a hostage," said the man, ignoring Cimarron's remark. "We'll kill her if you make a move against us—you or anyone else."

Cimarron saw the glint of the sharpened spoon in Jimmy's hand and the ugly, the eager, glint in the man's brown eyes. He stood without moving, his hands still held above his head.

"Let's get out of here, Maynard!" Sturgis urged, addressing the man who had just spoken to Cimarron.

And then the riders wheeled their three horses and went galloping toward the gate of the compound. Cimarron's hand dropped to his gun. He drew it. Raised it. Sighted along its barrel.

And then lowered it because the horses were traveling in a single file directly in front of him, Jimmy bringing up the rear, the woman hostage seated directly behind him.

He was about to move to the left to get a clear shot when, a flatbed wagon turned into the compound from Rogers Avenue. Cimarron, when the mounted men's single file went suddenly ragged as they avoided the wagon, fired, and the man riding alone toppled from his saddle and hit the ground, where he lay without moving.

A moment later, Charley Burns came out of the courthouse.

He drew his gun when Cimarron shouted, "Jailbreak!" but he didn't fire because the wagon and its driver was between him and his targets. Cimarron swung around and began to run, but before he could reach his horse, several prisoners appeared in the open outer door of the jail. He leveled his .44 at them and barked, "Back!"

He was joined a moment later by Burns and the two men herded the would-be jailbreakers back into the jail.

When the prisoners were safely confined and both jail doors had been locked, Burns turned to Cimarron and snapped, "How the hell did they get out?"

"It was your fault, Charley."

"My fault! What the hell do you mean it was my fault? You were in charge of the jail."

"That's just what I was getting at, Charley. It was your fault those bastards broke out on account of you went and let a careless, not to mention simpleminded, man take charge of your jail—namely, me."

"Where are you going?"

"To find out if that man I shot's still alive. If he is, he might be able to tell me something. I might be able to make him tell me something that'll put me on the trail of Sturgis and his friends. I've every intention of bringing those bastards back here to jail, where they all belong."

About the Author

LEO P. KELLEY was born and raised in Pennsylvania's Wyoming Valley and spent a good part of his boyhood exploring the surrounding mountains, hunting and fishing. He served in the Army Security Agency as a cryptographer, and then went "on the road," working as dishwasher, laborer, etc. He later joined the Merchant Marine and sailed on tankers calling at Texan, South American, and Italian ports. In New York City he attended the New School for Social Research, receiving a BA in Literature. He worked in advertising, promotion, and marketing before leaving the business world to write full time.

Mr. Kelley has published a dozen novels and has several others now in the works. He has also published many short stories in leading magazines.

JOIN THE CIMARRON READERS' PANEL

Help us bring you more of the books you like by filling out this survey and mailing it in today.

1. Book title:_____

   Book #:_____

2. Using the scale below how would you rate this book on the following features.

Poor		Not so Good			O.K.			Good		Excellent
0	1	2	3	4	5	6	7	8	9	10

                                                        Rating
Overall opinion of book..................................._____
Plot/Story ...._____
Setting/Location ...._____
Writing Style ...._____
Character Development ...._____
Conclusion/Ending ...._____
Scene on Front Cover ...._____

3. On average about how many western books do you buy for

   yourself each month?_____

4. How would you classify yourself as a reader of westerns?
   I am a (   ) light   (   ) medium   (   ) heavy   reader.

5. What is your education?
   (   ) High School (or less)   (   ) 4 yrs. college
   (   ) 2 yrs. college   (   ) Post Graduate

6. Age_____   7. Sex: (   ) Male   (   ) Female

Please Print Name_____

Address_____

City_____State_____Zip_____

Phone # (   )_____

Thank you. Please send to New American Library, Research Dept, 1633 Broadway, New York, NY 10019.

Ø

Exciting Westerns by Jon Sharpe from SIGNET

𝄞

Exciting Westerns by Jon Sharpe

Buy them at your local

bookstore or use coupon

on next page for ordering.

Ⓢ

Wild Westerns by Warren T. Longtree

**Buy them at your local
bookstore or use coupon
on next page for ordering.**